HOVERING

DOROTHY-JANE DANIELS

LUNA NOVELLA #7

Contents

Chapter One

On a sunny, blustery Sydney day, Zo drove over the bridge. The old campervan needed a service. It was too old for most places to repair; there was only one garage in Sydney that would look at it. The price wasn't worth it; they never used the campervan anymore, but it reminded her of holidays and younger kids and sand. The GPS was flickering in and out of usefulness, but Zo knew the way, or at least the general direction. She found the place at last, dealt with the prevarications and the head shaking and promised to be back in a few hours. It wasn't long before she was settled into a cafe with a book.

The barista was a short man covered in tattoos, who had greeted her like a long-lost older sister. He admired her dragonfly when he brought over her coffee. Zo was embarrassed to have the latest version; it suddenly seemed like showing off. A gift from her husband after a trip to Singapore, she was quick to say, but even that sounded pretentious. But the barista didn't seem to mind. They talked for a while about the way in which the flies had almost become pets – a strange hybrid between useful technology and companion. More personable than a phone. Zo's dragonfly settled on her table near the sugar.

Two cups and a piece of orange cake later the inevitable call came. The garage would need more time: parts had to be ordered, and could she pick it up tomorrow? Zo agreed. What else could she do? She thought about ways to get home, buses, the train, a taxi. There was a ferry at the end of the road, she thought. And then, on impulse, because she'd been staring at the brochure for the last hour, and because no-one else was home nor likely to be until later in the week, she left the cafe and walked downhill, following the map in the leaflet. The wind pulled at her, pushing her on, until she came to the house.

It wasn't the beautiful house the brochure had promised. Not anymore. The garden was overgrown, the paint was peeling. It looked so tired Zo decided it had probably been abandoned. It was close to the end of the street, with water nearby on two sides. Perhaps the foundations had already started to give; perhaps there was no hope.

The wind tugged at her, propelled her through the open gate and up the path to the front door. Three steps, swept and clean, if a little crumbly. A turquoise door. Still beautiful. With a brass knocker shaped like a whale's tail.

Zo was about to turn around, find a way back home, when the door opened.

A tall man who looked as if he had stepped from the pages of Moby Dick stood just inside. He had a greying beard and wore a knitted cap, though it didn't seem cold enough for that to Zo.

'You're wanting a room?' he asked.

'Yes,' said Zo. 'I saw your brochure.' She brandished it, a token of sanity. 'Just for tonight if you've got something.'

'I've a room at the top of the house if you're interested.'

Zo followed the owner through the foyer and up three flights of stairs. A young man opened a door on the second floor and walked past them, head down. There was a cluster of small stars tattooed on the back of his neck. At the top of the stairs, on the third floor, the man opened the door and stood back, as if expecting her delight. And he was right. The room itself was ordinary, though in better shape than the outside of the house, and it promised views. It had a bed and a dresser and all the other bits you might expect, but most of the room was dominated by a baby grand piano. Zo walked over to it, opened the lid, tried a few notes. Still reasonably in tune, with a beautiful touch. A Baldwin. An incredible discovery.

'I didn't expect a piano.'

'Belonged to my mother. Do you play?'

'I teach.'

'Play something.'

Zo sat and began the second movement of the Rachmaninoff before she'd had time to think. Normally she would have said no, made out-of-practice excuses, or claimed a lack of music. Somehow here she had nothing to lose. She played the intro, mixing the orchestral and the piano parts the way she usually did.

'Beautiful,' said the man. 'I'm Callum.'

'Zo.' She turned to look at him. 'Do you play too?'

'No, not at all,' said Callum. 'I'll let you be.'

Zo spread her hands. 'I've nothing,' she said. 'Just my car's being repaired, and I saw the brochure and the house seemed beautiful.' She stopped, realising that the man probably wanted to leave, wasn't at all interested in her decisions.

'You've a car?'

'A broken one. More of a campervan.'

'Could I borrow it? Just for an hour or so?'

'I guess so. It's old.' Zo saw the look on his face. 'But why not? It won't be ready until tomorrow, probably only in the afternoon.'

'That'll work.'

'I'll let you know when they call.' She smiled, uncertain.

'Come down later,' he said after a moment, 'and I'll make you dinner. But you could keep playing.'

He turned and left, leaving the door ajar.

Zo wanted to go back to the shops and get a few things. Soap, a toothbrush, something clean to wear. Why hadn't she thought of that before? Instead, she began the concerto again, letting the music flow over her and she managed, with only a few wrong notes and guesses, to play right until the end of the second movement. A foray to the shops, then, before it was too dark, before she changed her mind. And then she'd been promised dinner. She'd promised a car.

*

When Zo wandered downstairs, nobody seemed to be about. She found a room at the back with a large dining table and chairs and beyond that a kitchen which looked well-used and not overly clean. She retreated to the first room and saw comfortable chairs positioned close to the far wall. Beside them was a collection of what seemed to be giant insects made from old, heavy pieces of fabric. They were beautiful, dusty things. The dust added to their charm. She put a hand out to touch one.

'Careful.' The voice belonged to an old man dressed in an immaculately tailored suit which had seen better days. His grey hair was slicked back, but attempting to break away, and his glasses were yellowed and slightly skewwhiff. He took some of the insects down from the display, handed them to her one at a time. Moths, spiders, beetles. His fingers were bent, but sure.

'Are they yours?' Zo asked. 'They're lovely.'

'Make them, sell them. Hundred dollars a pop.'

A hundred dollars for a dusty moth seemed too much to Zo. 'I've not got that much on me,' she said.

'And no fly with you?'

'Of course, but I have a car in repair ...'

'I understand,' said the man, placing the creatures back, disappointed. She had let him down.

'Perhaps tomorrow, after I see what it all costs.' She held out a hand. 'I'm Zo.'

'Wirt.'

They shook hands and Wirt executed a small bow.

'He's given you the top room then.'

'Just for tonight.'

'Won't ever give it to me. And my creatures need the air; too much mould down here.'

'I'm not here for long, maybe that's why.'

'So you say.'

Zo thought about offering to have Wirt's insects up in her room. But Wirt would probably think she wanted to steal one. She was rescued by the arrival of Callum, the offer of a glass of wine, a discussion of dietary preferences and options.

'Build us a fire, Wirt,' said Callum. 'I'm off to cook.'

Callum disappeared into the kitchens and Wirt slowly built a fire, muttering all the while about the effect of smoke on his creations.

'Have you nowhere else to keep them?' asked Zo.

'Nowhere safe.'

'Could you bring in a cabinet? Store them away?'

'Had one once,' said Wirt. 'It disappeared.'

Zo understood things would always be difficult with Wirt, that there would be no solutions, only complaints. But the wine was soothing, and the surroundings had fallen into something like the ambience promised by the brochure now that the light was dimmer and there was food in the offing.

The smell of dinner cooking had other residents drifting in. Wirt busied himself setting the table. Places for eight, though so far only three others had turned up. A couple, a man and a woman, middle-aged and bound up together, and the young man with the stars on his neck. Zo smiled, but no-one introduced themselves.

The young man placed a casserole dish on the table. They served themselves while Callum introduced them: Tim was the young man's name; he managed a smile, nothing more. The woman was called Edda. She appeared to be the only other woman here, but Zo didn't detect any solidarity. Instead, she was ready for battle, her dress and cardigan, her hairpins and makeup all a form of armour. Reuben, her partner, was cautious and pleasant, but also slightly wary.

There wasn't much talk until the food on their plates had been devoured. Reuben looked longingly at the remains of the chicken casserole but didn't help himself to more. He held his left hand awkwardly and Zo could see the scars and the crooked bones jutting under the skin.

'It's just the one night you're here for?' asked Edda.

Zo thought she detected something of a threat.

'She said so already, didn't she?' remarked Wirt.

'Just making conversation, being polite.'

'What brought you to us, Zo?' asked Reuben.

'I saw a brochure in a cafe while I was waiting for my car. It turned out that it won't be ready until tomorrow, so I thought, why not? The house is so lovely.'

'Seems odd, not to go home,' said Edda.

It was odd, thought Zo, and hard to explain beyond the fact that she didn't feel like traipsing home and back again. 'There's no-one home at the moment, they're all away, so I guess I thought why not give myself a small holiday.'

'She feels the pull.'

'Don't start with that, Wirt.'

'It's only the truth.'

'I'm glad you found us,' said Reuben. He lifted his glass and they all followed suit. Edda reluctantly, Wirt with the air of toasting the dead. But still, Zo felt comfortable enough in this strange gathering. And it was only for tonight.

'She plays the piano,' said Callum.

'So I heard,' said Edda.

'Beautiful,' said Tim.

'Thank you,' replied Zo. 'I surprised myself by remembering it.'

'No wonder the house wanted her,' said Wirt.

'Enough,' said Edda. She stood, started gathering dirty plates. 'You set for eight,' she said to Wirt.

'He'll be back.'

'Who, me? But of course.' A man in a long, slightly dirty coat swept into the room, bringing the night with him. 'Greetings, all,' he said as he dished himself up a large serving of chicken and a mound of vegetables.

'This is Zo,' said Callum.

'And hello, Zo,' said the man.

'And this is Ivar,' Edda said. 'Be careful with him. He's not someone to trust.' She gathered up the casserole dish and removed it from the table.

'And a very good evening to you, Edda.'

The woman paused on her way to the kitchen. 'Where's my ring, then? The one you said you'd get cleaned, the one that hasn't made it back to me for three weeks.'

'In safe hands.'

'Yours.'

'My hands are always safe.'

'Zo's only here for the night,' said Reuben.

'Is that so?' asked Ivar.

'And she plays the piano,' said Tim.

'Does she now?'

Ivar winked at Zo but settled into his food. He had no interest in her or the reason she was here. Edda gave Reuben a poke and they both cleared the table of everything but Ivar's meal and the setting no-one had touched. Zo saw Edda put a finger on the fork and Callum shake his head. Perhaps it was a superstition, or an offering for the unexpected guest. Zo had always liked that idea, although surely she was the unexpected guest tonight.

'Will you play for us again?' asked Tim.

'Don't bother her now,' said Callum. He'd been silent

throughout the meal, scarcely eating that Zo had seen, although he'd poured wine for himself and for her.

Zo was glad of his intervention. The Rachmaninoff was the best thing she could play; anything else would be disappointing. But the look on Tim's face changed her mind. What a sad, yearning creature he was.

'Just something short,' she said and walked out of the room before any of them could stop her, up the three flights of stairs and to the piano. She comforted herself with the knowledge that anything they heard would be faint and far away. Debussy. That was wafty enough to cover some slips. Zo began the opening chords of *The Engulfed Cathedral*. She imagined the music trickling down the stairs to the people below. Probably no-one was listening. But the cathedral rose through the mist anyway.

Chapter Two

When Zo came back downstairs, most of the others had settled into the chairs near Wirt's creations. Ivar had disappeared. No-one commented on her piano playing. She talked to Callum, watched Tim practise card tricks. Occasionally he would show her one. Shyly, quietly, without any showmanship. She listened to Reuben's tales of his childhood and the roundabout journey which had brought him, finally, to this place and to Edda. Edda's past was not divulged. Callum told her it was strange that he was even here. Usually, he explained, he was out at sea, defending the oceans. Protecting the whales. The others seemed slightly embarrassed when he spoke of this. They turned their heads to the side and endured. Even Callum described his job in such a way as to make it small, mock himself. As if it was a foolish and indulgent project. But Zo could see it was the heart of him. The whole evening had all been so different to the usual conversations she had about children and house prices and dramas with renovations. So different to the night she would likely have spent watching television or reading. She'd never thought that the city was as geographically divided as people pretended it was, but here she was in an entirely new world.

But she'd forgotten to check in at home. She'd left Michael a message about the car earlier in the afternoon before she'd decided to stay. The girls were at camp and were unlikely to contact her. But Michael? He was away, overseas once again, and perhaps not even back from work yet, out with colleagues or too exhausted to care. She would ring tomorrow. She cleaned her teeth in the small bathroom on the other side of her stairs and checked her fly once more. No messages. She wandered over to the piano, could not resist a few quiet notes, but then she stripped off her clothes and pulled herself under the sheets. The final chords of the Debussy echoed in her head as she fell asleep.

In the morning, the house was quiet, as if no-one at all lived there. Zo crept into the kitchen, feeling like an intruder, but persevering nonetheless. She found an old coffee percolator and coffee in the fridge. She could see foodstuffs marked with people's names, mostly Edda's, and she wondered about the arrangements here. She'd thought it was more of a Bed and Breakfast, that the meal last night was part of the deal. The contents of the fridge suggested a boarding house. Still, they'd all sat and eaten Callum's food last night. And the coffee hadn't been named. She felt safe enough taking some.

The light streaming in through the kitchen windows made everything look old and shabby. Built-up grease on the stove and the stains on the floor. But there were clean mugs – black ones with a pirate logo. And the coffee, when it was done, was rich and bitter and just as it should be. She found sugar and a stash of spoons covered by delicately enamelled insect patterns. One was a cicada, another a butterfly, and Zo saw a spider and a wasp. She chose a moth. It was almost too beautiful for such mundane use.

'Is there more of that?' Callum stood in the doorway of the kitchen, the dark, faded communal room behind him. There was enough coffee for another cup, and she handed it to him, thinking he could add his own milk or sugar. He drank it as it was.

'Not myself before coffee,' he said.

'Me neither.' And then, realising that he might be up for a reason. 'The car won't be ready until later, I don't think.'

'Doesn't matter.' Callum went into the lounge room, pulled back blinds, opened curtains. Zo joined him, unsure but not certain what else to do. To have remained standing in the kitchen would be just as awkward. A set of three dice had been left on the table. Zo picked them up. They were covered in symbols: eyes, arrows, wands, stars. She turned them over, investigating, and then closed them inside her fist and shook them.

Callum grabbed her fist and lowered it to the table.

Zo opened her fingers, let the dice fall back onto the table. She was embarrassed, she didn't understand.

'You don't want to make a cast. Superstitious. Humour me.'

'Are they yours?'

'No. They belong to that young idiot, Tim.'

'The one who did card tricks? I liked him.'

'He thinks ... doesn't matter what he thinks. Let his stuff be.'

'I'm sorry, I didn't realise.'

Callum moved one shoulder dismissively.

'Have they been here long, your other guests?'

'Guests! Long enough.'

'Wirt seems to want my room for his creations.'

'Your room now, is it?' Zo thought, hoped, he might be teasing.

'He's worried about mould, I think.'

'He's worried about everything, that bugger. Not that he's wrong to worry, but they're safe enough here.'

'Is it safe, the house I mean?'

Callum looked up, straight at her. 'Safe?'

'I mean the foundations. You're close to the water. Lots of people have had trouble.'

Callum brushed her words away with a sweep of his arm. 'She's solid. I'm just not here often enough to take proper care of her.'

'It's a beautiful house.'

'That it is.' But Callum was already standing, on his way out. 'Help yourself to whatever food. I'm not much good in the morning.'

Callum nodded, walked away. Zo couldn't help but feel she'd offended him. She thought about breakfast, decided that the kitchen was too difficult to negotiate further. She looked at the dice, was tempted to pick them up and throw them, just out of curiosity, or perversity, but the floor creaked and when she turned around Tim was there. She smiled and his face lightened. All at once another person.

'There's coffee if you want some,' she offered, realising too late there were probably only dregs by now.

Tim dipped into the kitchen, rattled and procured and returned to Zo.

'Was there enough?'

He nodded, something else on his mind. 'What was that

piece you played last night?' he asked.

'Debussy,' she said. *'The Engulfed Cathedral.'*

'Why'd you choose that one?'

'I could remember it. There's not a lot I can play without the music.' And it had seemed right, thought Zo. But that might sound ridiculous. She saw that Tim had drawn the dice towards him and folded them into a pocket while they were talking.

'What are they?' she asked.

'Nothing. I shouldn't have left them here.' Tim's face retreated into itself.

Zo would have liked to have asked more. Got to know him a little better. He seemed too young to be living in a place like this. And how could he afford it unless he had a job?

'I liked your card tricks last night,' she said.

'Thanks,' he said, without looking up from his coffee. 'I could cast for you,' he said. 'With the dice, I mean.'

Zo thought of Callum taking her hand in his fist, lowering quickly to the table. 'Is it safe?' she wanted to ask. But it seemed harmless, it seemed something to offer Tim.

'OK. Tonight?' She probably wouldn't be here tonight, although she supposed she could hang around for a while, if it really meant that much to him.

'Now,' said Tim, 'before the others come down.' He seemed insistent, yet also expecting her to refuse him.

'Tim ...' Zo didn't know how to phrase her question. It was easier just to agree. 'OK then.'

'You need to hold them,' he said. Zo didn't like to say she'd already picked them up. He handed her the three dice and she felt foolish and guilty. 'Shake and throw.'

Zo let the dice fall onto the table. Each displayed the same face: beautiful curling clouds. Underneath each cloud were dashes of rain.

'Oh,' said Tim. 'That can't be right. Not all the same. I thought… I thought it would be something better.'

'What does it mean?'

'They're rain clouds,' began Tim. There was obviously something more, something he didn't want to tell her. 'It must be wrong; I made you do it too fast.' Before he could say anything further, they heard footsteps. Tim scooped the dice into his pocket.

'Any news about the car?' asked Callum.

'Not yet.'

'Sure,' said Callum. And he disappeared back to wherever he had been. When Zo turned around, Tim was already in the kitchen. He'd taken both her mug and his to wash up. He and his cloudy dice were lost to her.

Chapter Three

Zo saw the babies before she saw anything else, wrapped packages bobbing through the water. When she realised what they were, she ran. How had this happened? So many of them, all at once? But then she saw the adults. Men and women both, waist deep, waiting to collect the babies as they completed their short, lonely journey. She slowed when she saw a woman come out of a house with an overflowing garden, making her way through the pumpkin vines and the lemongrass on the verge.

She'd admired the garden before on one of her walks. Two days now, and no word from the garage. The only thing keeping her here was her promise to Callum.

The woman's baby was wrapped in a package of woven leaves. Just like an expensive soap, or a basket of flowers. The woman wore gumboots and faded, once black jeans. She looked across at Zo and smiled.

'Couldn't find my wetsuit,' she said. 'This will have to do.'

'What is this?' Zo tried to keep her tone steady.

'Moses day. So the babies won't fear the water.'

The woman lifted a hand and walked away, hurrying to

get to the ceremony. They were singing now. Happy songs, peaceful, calming. And the babies were soothed. None were crying and some were gurgling.

It was an act of hope, that the water levels were manageable, that the harbour wouldn't become too high, too much. This was the new world now. They had to accept it, become as close to water creatures as they could. The woman with the leaf wrapped baby walked out into the water to meet the others. She kissed her child on the forehead and then laid her down, letting her bob for a little while, testing, Zo thought, to see if the parcel was truly waterproof. And then, with a gentle push, she let the child go. To whom? Zo wondered. To anyone standing on the other side. As long as they were afloat the babies were in no real danger. And even if they began to sink, they could be easily retrieved. Zo didn't think she'd have been able to let go of her daughters so easily.

The woman turned to her and waved. 'Come in,' she called.

'I'm not dressed,' said Zo. Although she had already kicked off her shoes, Zo rolled up her jeans as far as she could. She walked over the rocks to the water's edge and hesitated, but the singing drew her, and she found herself standing knee-deep in water. A man wearing a wetsuit turned to greet her. 'This next one's for you,' he said. Zo watched the package drift closer. This baby's coracle was made of thick, white plastic. She watched the child closely, wished it happiness, wisdom, protection. And when it was close, she scooped it out of its plastic shell and cradled it. The wetsuit man held on to the coracle.

'You'll need to send her back,' he said after a moment. Zo put her baby back in its container, gave it a gentle push and watched. It was mostly women, but some men, one very elderly man. They all seemed calm; they all were singing. Zo wondered again if she could have done it.

And then another child was passed to her. The water was full of babies. Babies of all shapes and sizes. One was fussing in his or her container. Another seemed to be completely asleep. Zo felt tears well up, the kind of tears that had sprung unawares when she'd watched her daughter dance or at surprising moments in otherwise boring school productions.

And then there were no more children washing towards them. The last of the babies returned to their family and the songs drifted into their final notes. Zo followed the wetsuit man back to the shore. Her jeans were heavy and cold. She felt foolish with no family to talk to, no baby to hold.

'You went in!' It was the woman with the leaf wrapped baby.

Zo looked down at her jeans. 'Yes, it was wonderful, but now I'm soaked.'

The woman waved her objections away, showed her the coracle she had made. 'Look, totally dry!' Zo made effusive noises. 'I used water lily. Lots of layers. And tested it. You have no idea, a crazy woman floating leaf boats in the bath. Sorry, I'm raving. My name's Kyra.' The woman stuck out her hand.

'Zo.' She grasped the hand and the woman clasped it.

'Thank you for coming in.'

'It was my pleasure.'

Kyra looked at Zo in a way that seemed like friendly assessment. 'Do you live nearby?' she asked. 'I think I've seen you around.'

'Just for the moment.' It seemed too difficult to explain further, foolish to admit that she was stuck here because she had promised to lend someone a car that was still being repaired.

'I'm taking Beattie home for a sleep now, but why don't you visit some time? You know, the house with the garden, where we met?'

'I'd love to.'

Kyra danced back up to the street, still euphoric, thought Zo. She wasn't sure the invitation was genuine. She wouldn't be here for that much longer. But the warmth of the greeting lifted her up and through the crowds. She walked back to the house, ready for someone to laugh at her wet jeans, expecting Ivar, at least, to materialise and mock her, but no-one was there. Up in her aerie, she changed and hung her wet clothes up to dry with a towel underneath to catch the drips.

She sat on the bed and checked her fly. Nothing. Callum seemed prepared to wait; she hoped he wouldn't be disappointed. It had only been a couple of days, after all. And for an old car, that was nothing. But now she was restless. She felt like singing, she felt as if she could jump out of the window and fly. She would shop, find food to cook for them all, repay Callum's hospitality. And Tim. He needed feeding, she thought.

*

Zo hadn't meant to come back so late, but the night had caught her unawares. She'd spent too much time fussing at the unfamiliar shops and she'd wandered home slowly, captured by the dark blue evening sky and the wheeling of birds in the last of the light. Even the trees seemed something magical. It wasn't even that late, only around six. There was no need to be scared, not this early. But she still started when she felt a pull at her coat.

'Missus, Missus, something for us?' It was almost a hiss.

'No,' she said, then realised she shouldn't have spoken because now there were at least five creatures in front of her. Hunched figures, small, like goblins. She kept walking, keeping her steps as firm and as solid as possible. Fast, but not hurried, not afraid.

And then two of them by her side, one grabbing at each arm. They were as tall as her, easily, but still she thought of them as children. To be pitied, not to be feared. A hand snaked into her pocket, and she tried to brush it away. She was only a few houses from home. She could make it. They hadn't tried to grab the bag filled with groceries. She'd have gladly let them have it.

'Get away from her.'

Ivar. She only recognised him by his voice. He took two great steps forward, looming, and the goblins scattered, although only a few steps away.

'No harm, no harm.'

'Better not be,' said Ivar. 'And hand it back.'

A flurry of feet and her wallet was returned to her by one hand, her fly by another.

'Anything else?'

A chorus of no, but Ivar looked at Zo. She shook her head, too embarrassed to remember if there'd been anything else in her pockets.

Ivar grabbed one from the shadows, took a parcel from a wriggling body, not something Zo recognised, and then let the goblin go. He growled, a mock growl, pretend, but it worked, and the creatures scattered right back and away.

He took her elbow, hurried her back home. She was glad of it, though she shook him off as soon as the door was closed behind them.

'Thank you,' she managed. 'Who are they?'

'Just kids. It's a joke to them. A game. You have to know the rules.'

'I thought they were goblins at first.'

'Yeah, that's likely. Just undernourished humans.'

'They need food?'

'They've got food. Just forget to eat.'

'Maybe—'

'You can't help them, Zo.'

She wanted to say more, but the door opened and Reuben came in. There was a rush of cold and night and it carried Ivar up the stairs and away. Reuben gave her a half-smile and then disappeared, leaving Zo alone. She didn't want to go inside; she felt as if there was something unfinished in the foyer. There were letters in Callum's mail slot. She wanted to pull out the letters, look, see what kind of mail he received. Only the thought that she might be caught stopped her.

She took her food to the kitchen, made her curry, half thinking of offering some to Ivar's goblins. Edda and Reuben came in together. They watched her cook and Reuben regaled her with a funny, if long-winded, anecdote about room choices. It seemed to Zo that this was a debate that had begun long ago and, perhaps, would never find an end. Reuben wanted to swap places with Ivar, or for Edda to swap with Tim, but Ivar wouldn't budge and, claimed Edda, neither would Tim. Zo thought the woman probably wanted her own space, her privacy. She understood that. A better romance from afar. Even if it was only a floor.

They took the food out to the dining room table and Wirt drifted in. He was an old man; everything about him was battered and crumpled. Fading but still functional. But he ate great dollops of Zo's curry. She would have liked to have fed Tim, but he didn't come down. Ivar turned up, helped himself. Gave her a nod and a grin of thanks. The leftovers she put in the fridge. She suspected they would be gone by tomorrow.

Chapter Four

The door of Tim's room was open. The last time Zo had seen him, he'd been sitting on a rock by the water, practising his tricks, cards running through his hands like sand. But that had been several days ago. She was stranded now. The car was ready at last, but Callum had taken it, fetched it from the garage himself, with promises to return as soon as he could. Zo was surprised by how little she cared.

She stood in the doorway, called his name softly. No answer. The room was too small, too cluttered for him to hide, and she felt suddenly ashamed of the large room she'd been granted at the top of the house. This room was full of books and paraphernalia. An empty bird cage sat on a rickety table. Inside the cage was a book, a pack of cards, and the three dice Zo had thrown. Faded and slightly ripped posters covered the walls. Above the bed was a copy of a black-and-white photograph, showing mermaids resting on the beach. They were obviously actresses taking a break from filming, back before there was CGI, back when suggestion was enough for the imagination. Why did Tim love it? Because it was so obviously not real?

'He's not there.' Ivar was standing on the stairs behind her.

'He hasn't been around for days.'

'He's a big boy.'

'He's—'

'He doesn't need a mother.'

'He needs someone; everyone needs someone.'

'Yeah, but you're going home soon, right? You won't be here much longer.'

'As soon as Callum brings the car back.'

'Right.'

'Does Tim go away often?' she asked. Mostly to bring the conversation back on track.

'Don't keep tabs. He'll be fine, don't worry.'

'Even though his door's open?'

'Hungry?' asked Ivar.

'Sure,' said Zo. She'd thought vaguely about lunch, but she didn't really want to go to the kitchen and find all the food she'd cooked yesterday already eaten.

'Follow me.'

'OK. Let me grab—'

'No, no, lunch is on me.' Ivar executed a bow which managed to mock both himself and Zo.

'Then let me change. Brush my hair.'

'Two minutes. But it's nothing fancy. Don't get all excited.'

They walked for several blocks. Zo felt awkward trying to keep in step with Ivar's long strides and restless turnings. Despite his spikiness, she usually felt comfortable around him. But out in the daylight, away from the house, she found she had nothing to say. She was walking beside a stranger dressed in an old, slightly grubby coat.

And then, around the corner from a row of cafes and restaurants Zo wasn't dressed for, Ivar danced up four concrete steps. This place was a different thing. Everything mismatched, gleaned from somewhere else and painted. Artwork on the walls, some hanging from the ceiling. One wall was covered by a copy of Hokusai's Great Wave. Someone was playing banjo in the corner by the window. Real, live music. The room smelled of coffee, burnt sugar and pumpkin soup. On one wall, close to the banjo player, were coloured plastic circles attached to hooks. Ivar was standing close to them, listening to the banjo player.

'Blue for soup and a roll, red for coffee, purple for a cakey thing, green for the full complete meal,' said Ivar.

'Blue, I guess,' said Zo.

Ivar took a blue and a green circle down as well as two reds. 'Good coffee,' he said. The woman at the counter knew him, greeted him with a grin and a joke. 'And this is Zo,' he told her.

'Nice to meet you.' The woman smiled but didn't offer her name.

They sat, no table number. Coffee arrived almost instantly, and lunch was brought out before long. Steaming pumpkin soup with a multigrain roll and butter on the side. Ivar's meal was chicken with pine nuts and oranges with a side of roast veggies.

'Thank you,' said Zo. 'This is lovely.'

'And now you can come any time,' said Ivar.

'Well, maybe,' said Zo, thinking of the money she had already spent on accommodation and food, feeling slightly guilty that she'd indulged herself. She'd even bought some new clothes, nothing much, but it was all adding up.

Ivar looked at her, took a great mouthful of chicken, chewed, sat back. 'It's all free, you know.'

'Free?' Zo had seen people pay. There were people there now, bringing out cards, some sending their flies. She'd thought Ivar must have an understanding with the people here.

'With the tokens, it's free. Idea is, if you're in the money, you buy a token for someone who needs a bit of a leg up.'

'Have you ever bought a token?'

'Nup.'

'You introduced me. I've never met them before and this is the first thing I do, get free food.'

'That's the whole point of the system.'

Zo shook her head.

'So you're too good for this?'

'I could afford to pay. I don't need someone to pay for me.'

'Not for long. Not if you keep cooking for everyone and nobody else shares.'

'I'll be going home soon.'

'Maybe, maybe not.'

Zo was stung by the thought that Ivar thought her incapable of making money. She used to have some piano students, though not many, not enough to survive on. She'd let them drift away. And none of them would have travelled here. She found herself thinking what it might be like if she stayed, how she would afford it. 'I could teach the piano.'

'That won't even pay the rent.'

'It might. One day.'

'Just what I need. A whole lot of people traipsing up the stairs banging out more of that classical shit.'

'I'll be gone soon, Ivar. Don't worry. Callum will bring the car back and I'll go home.'

'So you say.' He drained his cup, leaned back. 'Wanna see something weird?' he asked.

Zo wondered what he usually did with his day. He seemed to have time this morning. Time to waste on her. But this was unusual; usually he had an air of distraction, of business going on somewhere in the back of his head at least. He was waiting for something, she thought, and she was a way of passing the time.

'Sure,' she said.

'It's a bit of a walk.'

'I can walk.'

They set off through streets that grew gradually less cared for. Some homes seemed too derelict to house anyone safely. They came to an abandoned lot. Ivar held back a section of mesh fence that, to judge by the rust, had been cut long ago. They walked over concrete and tattered grass through to a building several storeys high. Most of it was covered in graffiti. Tags and slogans, but one wall featured a large portrait of a man standing in an umbrella and floating over an ocean filled with sea creatures. The umbrella did not seem enough protection from the tentacles and teeth. To his left were gaps that seemed to be the remains of an old car park. There was something about it that niggled at Zo's brain.

'Oh, I know this,' she said. 'I've been here. Ages ago. This was a shopping centre. Wasn't there some explosion, or a storm or something, that made it unsafe?'

'Yep.'

They kept walking. Zo looked up at the building, trying

to spot areas of collapse or places that might be hazardous. It all seemed solid, although the only inhabitants appeared to be birds.

Ivar leant against what seemed to be a sturdy metal door with his right shoulder. The door groaned open, and he slipped through. Zo hesitated until an impatient rap at the door made her follow.

It took a while to adjust to the light. But gradually Zo realised that they were in the bowels of the shopping centre. The part that was purely functional, that nobody had ever bothered to make glamorous. Graffiti had made its way inside, but the building was surprisingly clean. If Zo had thought about it, she might have expected rubbish, or urine and vomit. Animal nests or detritus. But now that they had travelled for a while, this part of the building seemed to have the air of a well-worn path, as much as the footpath she and Ivar had been on not long ago.

Another door, this one opened by Ivar's flat hand, and then into a wide-open space. Light fell in from the clear roof several storeys up. Patterns danced on the walls. The air was moist and expectant. The shopping centre had transformed into an urban lake. There was enough room to walk around the edge, but otherwise the space was filled with water. Ivar was standing very still and when Zo joined him, he put a hand on her arm.

'Look,' he said.

In the water were fish. Flickers of orange, yellow and black. They swirled like birds, although their movement was calm and more measured.

'Wonderful,' whispered Zo.

'Time to say hello,' said Ivar. He moved to the right, following the narrow concrete strip that bordered the lake. A group of men were sitting up ahead. They flickered in and out of existence as the light caught the water in different ways. As she came closer, she saw that they were all at least middle-aged. Old clothes, grey hair, various ethnicities. She felt awkward as she approached them. Not that they were unfriendly, but they were assessing her. Her presence here, her association with Ivar. There were no welcoming smiles.

'Hello.' Zo spoke to break the silence.

'This is Zo,' said Ivar. 'She's been drawn to the house.' Several of the men nodded at her. Another dipped his net into the water and drew out a long, orange fish which he placed in a Styrofoam box. Zo could hear it flapping around in distress. No names were offered in return.

'How long?' asked one of the men.

'Ten days or so,' said Ivar.

There were more nods. Gestures Zo couldn't interpret. She thought of telling them about the car.

'She can still leave,' said another man. This one was older than the rest. Or he appeared to be. His hair was completely grey, as was his long beard, the tips of which trailed in the water.

Heads were shaken, differing opinions were muttered.

And then one of them moved his arm to the side. 'Would you like to sit down?' he asked.

'Thank you,' said Zo.

She sat cross-legged, collapsing down where she stood. Another man poured her a drink out of a Thermos and offered it to her. She sipped it to be polite. It was tea, only tea.

And he smiled when he saw her surprise.

Ivar sat too, as if resigned to whatever rituals might be required.

'You could take her back,' said the old one.

'She doesn't want to go,' said Ivar.

'I'm waiting for my car,' offered Zo. Despite herself and because she wanted them to talk to her directly.

'Don't,' said the oldest man.

'You have a home,' said another. 'Go to it.'

'I've told her,' said Ivar.

'Do you feed them?' asked Zo. 'The fish?'

'No need,' said the man with the net. 'In the beginning, yes, but now ... It's self-sustaining. Its own ecosystem.'

'Just take the big ones out,' said another.

'And let the little ones grow.'

They all chuckled, though Zo didn't understand the joke. Her arm was nudged, and she found her mug filled up with tea. 'Thank you so much.'

'She plays the piano,' said Ivar.

'Can you sing?' asked the man with the tea.

'No, no. My voice is all wrong. I mean. I can sing in tune, but no, I'm not a singer.'

'Sing us something,' said the oldest man.

'Oh,' said Zo, 'you really don't want to hear me sing.'

'Alright then.'

She felt them turn away from her, although there was no discernible movement. The water slapped gently against the side of the concrete.

'Go on,' said the man with the tea. 'Anything you like.'

All the songs Zo could think of were wrong. Inappropriate

songs about lost loves and yearning. And then she thought of *Blackbird*. It was short, at least, and she thought she knew all the words, though she would have liked to have sung a more watery song. She began, the first leap shaky but then, when the men seemed not to mind, she went on. Her voice gained strength, echoing on the concrete and then floating up over the water and into the empty shopping centre above her. Like singing in the bathroom, she thought. A bathroom full of fish and crazy men. She let the last notes drift over them and then smiled. No-one clapped, but some of them smiled back.

'Thank you,' said the man with the tea. 'Quite beautiful.'

Ivar stood. 'We should go,' he said.

Zo drank the rest of the tea and handed the cup back to her friend. 'Another time, a longer song?' he asked.

'I'll practise,' said Zo. And, in that moment, she meant it.

He pressed a small packet into her hand. Tea, Zo thought. 'While you wait.'

'Thank you.'

Ivar lifted his arm in farewell and then strode towards the outside world.

Zo waved too, but they were all looking away, absorbed by the fish or in their own conversations. One of them was reading. Another appeared to be looking at a tablet.

She ran to catch up with Ivar. She wanted to thank him for showing her the fish, but he seemed too grumpy to speak to. And he was walking so fast that it took all her energy to keep him in view.

Only once they were out of the building and into the sunlight did he slow down.

'How long since you shopped here?' he asked.

'I don't know. A year or two.'

'And you think all those fish could turn up in a year or two?'

'Maybe it was longer.'

'Want me to take you home, back to your own house?' Something about the way he said it seemed very deliberate, although he wasn't looking at her. He kicked at an old Solo can by his feet.

Zo didn't want to say no. He was so obviously trying to help, trying to tell her something. But she couldn't say yes. She didn't know quite why. It was the sensible thing to do, the obvious thing. She could leave her number for Callum. She could come back and collect the campervan. She didn't even need it. She could give it to him, and it wouldn't matter. She was never going to use it again. They'd reached the mesh fence and Ivar held it open for her.

'You don't have to say anything, Zo. You know the offer's there, OK,' he said, still not looking at her, still keeping it casual. But she felt as if he was offering her something vital and important. A safety measure of some sort.

'OK.' Zo looked at him then, so that he would know she meant it. 'Thank you. For today and everything.'

'You keep saying thank you.'

'It's polite.'

'There's not that much to be thankful for.'

Chapter Five

When Zo got back to the house, she went straight to her room. Ivar had hived off early, leaving her to walk the last few blocks alone. She'd thought about dropping in on Kyra, but she wanted to reach the safety of her room. She put the packet of tea in the top drawer of her small bedside table. The piano was open and music had been placed on the stand.

A song, Zo saw. Nothing she knew. The accompaniment was easy enough for her to both play and sing without difficulty. Though she sang softly, almost under her breath. It had been a long time since she'd done this, sight sung an unknown song, but the melody drifted into her and out and she did not feel the need to check her notes against the surety of the piano.

The words seemed nonsense. Dragonflies and water lilies and rippled fish darting in and out. It would have been the song to sing to those men in the shopping centre lake. There was something English about it, something different to the Australian landscape. Almost innocent, except for the pull. As if it were the words of someone drowning. Not struggling but finding themselves further and further under the water without meaning to. Not realising until too late that there was no escape. But it was beautiful, if sad. Zo had just begun the second verse when she heard a cough at the door.

She turned. Edda was there, the look on her face unreadable. 'Tim's back. Reuben thought you'd like to know.'

'Thanks,' said Zo. 'I was a little worried. Though that's probably silly.'

'No,' said Edda. 'We all need someone to pull us back.'

Zo felt herself shake. A shudder, a foreboding. She needed food, that was all.

'Would you like a cup of tea?' she asked Edda. A gesture of friendship. But Edda was gone, her footsteps on the stairs.

Zo followed at a distance, not wanting to intrude. She peered inside Tim's room when she went down, but there was no sign of him. It wasn't until she was downstairs that she thought Edda might have been teasing, but there was Tim, sitting at the table writing. A pack of cards sat beside him.

'Hungry?' asked Zo.

'Always.' Tim glanced up and over and a quick smile flitted across his face.

Zo found bread in the kitchen which she knew she'd bought as well as jam and honey. She made a pile of toast and two cups of coffee and took them out. Tim closed his journal as soon as she came in, though Zo glimpsed a strange, curved script that looked like piles of pebbles. She offered Tim the food and he demolished several slices of toast and gulped coffee. And then, restored, he picked up the cards.

'Watch,' he told her.

He fanned the cards out and turned them so Zo could see them. They were ordinary playing cards with simple, modern graphics. He turned them towards him so that she could see their red backs and then pushed them into a pack. He fanned them again and showed her. This time slowly, deliberately. These cards were old. Their designs were intricate and there were marks that seemed like water stains.

'Choose one,' he said.

Zo closed her eyes, trying to enter into the spirit of the trick. She held out her hand, felt a card leap into her fingers.

She opened her eyes and suppressed a gasp. This was a queen. The queen of clubs, a dark-haired, cunning and malevolent manifestation. And not just a head and shoulders but a complete body. She appeared to be standing in shallow water. Vines and flowers twined through her hair. Zo put the card on the table, pretending to show Tim, but wanting it out of her hands.

'I thought so,' said Tim, and he gathered it up and put it back in the pack. He shuffled the pack and Zo could see that the cards had returned to their generic state.

'That's clever,' she said, trying to make it ordinary. Trying not to remember the look in the queen's eyes.

'They're old, the ones I showed you,' said Tim. 'I found them here, in the house.'

'How old does that make them?'

Tim shrugged. 'Maybe one hundred years, maybe more.' He looked down at them. 'They're beautiful,' said Zo, slowly, 'but a bit ...'

'Creepy? Yeah, I know. But they're not too bad. They're just caught up in their strange ways. They don't mean any harm.'

Zo wasn't sure that was so. 'Where have you been?' she asked. 'We missed you.' She hadn't meant to say anything, but she wanted to draw him back to the real world. Make sure he was safe and grounded.

'I wander,' said Tim. 'Sometimes walking helps me think. My room seems too small. And sometimes I need to get away.'

He looked at Zo as if he wanted her to understand without him saying more. She did understand if he meant the other people in the house. They were all older than him, hardly the most exciting companions. But she worried that he had meant something else. Something to do with the cards. Something to do with the house itself.

'I always come back,' he said.

Zo couldn't tell if that made him happy or sad.

The sound of hard, quick footsteps startled them both.

Edda stood at the end of the table, looking down at the cards then across at Zo. 'Party tricks,' she said. 'You're not taken in, are you?'

Zo looked across at Tim. Of course, she didn't think this was real magic, as unsettling as the illustration had been. Tim gathered the cards, putting them away and out of Edda's sight.

'He just thought I might be interested,' said Zo.

Edda lifted an arm to adjust her hair and Zo glimpsed old scars crisscrossing her forearm. Edda caught her look, almost put the arm down, but then kept it up, defiantly, Zo thought, daring her to comment. I understand more about life than you, the gesture said.

Tim stood, dragging his chair back. He glanced at Zo quickly with a half-smile and then left.

'There's coffee,' Zo told Edda.

Edda sat, poured herself a drink, took a sip. Zo finished the rest of hers, steeling herself to leave, feeling glued to the seat. Politeness had trapped her; she didn't know how to get away. Edda took a sip of the coffee, grimaced, but kept drinking. 'It's probably a bit cold,' said Zo. Edda waved her hand dismissively. 'He can't be helped,' she said. 'He's already in the grip of it.'

'I don't think he needs help. I just think he needs a friend.'

'You?'

'Somebody.'

'It will pull you in too if it hasn't already.'

'Have you seen the cards?' asked Zo.

'Of course.'

'Do you believe they're as old as Tim thinks?'

Edda dipped her head in assent.

'I understand that Tim seems caught up in them. Obsessed. But how can they hurt?'

'Any obsession is hurtful,' said Edda.

'Not always,' replied Zo, thinking of artists, inventors, great discoveries.

'And what will this one lead to?'

'He wants to find something wondrous,' said Zo. 'I did too when I was his age.'

'He will grow out of it,' said Edda.

'Maybe.' Although that was not what Zo meant. She remembered the longing for something more than the everyday. It still struck her now, although not as often and not as intensely. Or perhaps she didn't allow the intensity to overtake her. Growing older wasn't so much about losing emotion as developing a mask. Her husband, her children, her neighbours, the school mothers, the people at the shops, her students. None of those people expected her awash with great emotions and chasms. She couldn't let that sort of thing out. She didn't know anybody who did. 'Perhaps he'll find something that fills the need.'

'Fall in love.'

Zo smiled. It usually worked. It would pull him out of himself if nothing else. She heard a creak, perhaps someone else coming into the room, and turned, but there was no-one there. When she turned back to Edda, she was gone too. The whole room was deserted, as if it had been for years. Dust was floating down through streams of light creeping in through the cracked windows. Some of the chairs were on the floor, broken. The coffee pot and cups were still on the table, but the coffee had long evaporated and a dead insect lay, legs up, in her cup. The door to the kitchen was closed and looked as if it had fused to the surrounds. The walls were covered in patches of grey-green mould. Wirt's creations had decayed to almost nothing, although there was one moth, tip tilted on the edge of a shelf which seemed about to fly towards her.

The floor felt spongy beneath Zo's feet. Much of it had rotted away, leaving her and the table precariously poised over a dirty stretch of water. She daren't move. To stand might be to place too much pressure on the boards.

Zo twisted in her chair, looking behind her. A few metres back, the floorboards appeared intact. The door to the room was open and she could see light through it as if the front door was also ajar. If she could manage to leap across the rotten section, she could get out and away. She turned back, bracing herself to stand and to jump. But the room had righted itself. Edda was sitting, watching her. Zo's coffee cup was half full and there were no insects anywhere on the table. The paint on the walls was unblemished by mould, a little faded, but still elegant.

'You think he should fall in love,' repeated Edda.

'Why not? Zo stood, walked away, taking her cup with her. She threw the remains of her coffee in the kitchen sink, grasped the cold metal and steadied herself. She was tired, that was all, tired and the thought of Tim and his old cards had stirred her imagination. Or Edda had played a trick of her own. Zo wouldn't be surprised. She stayed in the kitchen a moment more then walked out, past Edda and away, back up to her own room.

Chapter Six

Zo decided to visit Kyra. It wasn't something she'd normally do, visit a casual acquaintance, but she wanted to shrug off the house, Edda in particular. She would take the tea the man at the shopping centre lake had given her. She could ask Kyra what sort of tea she thought it was. It could be an offering, an excuse. She needed a friend.

It wasn't late enough to be cold yet, but when Zo opened the front door, a blast of wind shot up and through and made her run back upstairs for her coat. Not hers, exactly. Something she had found hanging up in her room. She hadn't brought one with her. Autumn hadn't really come in yet, but sometimes in the evening a chill would rise in the house that made Zo glad of the extra layer. She'd worried about showing herself in it at first, afraid that it had belonged to some older, more loved member of the household, but no-one had commented. And now the coat almost seemed hers. It was black. Long enough to reach her hips and with a hood at the back. The cut was good, and it fitted Zo well, but the overall effect was unassuming. The metal buttons were engraved with leaves and, when you noticed them, were beautiful. But the coat was warm and comforting. It should have been too warm, but somehow it never was.

Zo pulled the front door open again. A swirl of leaves swept into the foyer but then the wind swept back around, and the door tried to close itself again. Zo held onto it. The sky had darkened, and it had begun to spit. She reached for an umbrella in the stand, lost her hold on the door, wrestled it open again. The wind poured into the house. When she pulled the front door shut, the metal door knocker bashed against the wood, as if it really were attached to an angry whale. Zo pushed the umbrella open against the wind, hoping it wouldn't flip right open and break. But by the time she was down the steps and onto the front path, the wind had gone, although the rain had picked up. She fiddled with the latch of the metal garden gate, trying to persuade it open. She was at the point of thinking she would jump across when the latch gave and hurled her out onto the footpath.

Zo looked back. 'OK,' she said to the house. 'That's enough. I'll come back. I ...' She'd almost said promise, but at the last moment, some superstitious part of her stopped her. She paused for a moment, looking at the wild, overgrown garden with twigs and sticks scattered across the front lawn. Then Zo trudged up the street. Kyra's garden looked untroubled, peaceful in the rain, green and fertile. So unlike Zo's abortive attempts to grow something edible at home.

She knocked on the door, reaching into the pocket of her coat for the tea. She rehearsed her greeting, worried that Kyra would feel this visit was an intrusion. She thought of making an excuse of the wind, pleading shelter, but the wind now seemed something she had dreamed up. She was just about to turn around, go back to the house, or keep on, up to the shops, when the door opened and there was Kyra, towel wrapped around her head, bare feet, faded track pants and an old jersey on which Zo could make out the word netball, but not the name of the club.

'Zo!' she cried.

Zo was glad Kyra had remembered her name. 'Sorry, I've got you out of the shower, I just—'

'Don't say sorry. Come in!' Kyra almost pushed her inside. Zo followed her down the hall and into the open space at the back of the house.

'I was given some tea,' said Zo. 'And I thought you might know what it was.'

Zo held out the packet and Kyra swooped on it. She opened the paper wrap and sniffed. 'Not sure,' she said. 'Can we drink it?'

'Of course,' said Zo.

Kyra put on water to boil, fetched a teapot and carefully scooped some of the tea leaves. The rest she parcelled up and gave back to Zo. 'Something special. Don't waste it all on me.' While they waited for the tea to infuse, Kyra bent over and towelled her hair dry. Zo watched as black curls erupted.

Kyra laughed when she saw her expression. 'Wild, huh? When I was younger, I used to straighten it all the time. Now ... Now I just let it free. Or try to tame it with a band.'

'You remind me of my daughter.' Zo had been caught by a memory of her own child coming out of the bathroom, towel falling from her head, fussing with her hair.

'Ah,' said Kyra, 'baby Beattie.' She'd heard the cry before Zo had. Kyra's baby seemed a peaceful child. Even her cry was a gentle alert. Zo's children had been squally and demanding. But she remembered the feel of a young child, pressed close as they slept in her bed. Completely asleep now that they were with her. The nightmares gone; the aloneness of the night banished. Her husband had hated it, always pulled the sheets and blankets towards him, muttering in his sleep, complaining about the lack of space. Although Zo had been the one who'd woken with a sore back and cramped muscles. She hadn't minded though. It had felt as if everyone was in their right place. But that time was over, and those children had grown up and away.

Kyra settled Beattie while Zo poured the tea. She found milk and honey and Kyra nodded for both. The baby sat in a tall chair, imbibing squashed banana and chewing on a biscuit. Kyra closed her eyes and smelled the drink. 'Cinnamon and ginger, definitely. Star Anise.'

'It's just a Chai.' Zo felt foolish. Nothing that she couldn't have made herself.

Kyra took a sip. 'Well, it's a very nice Chai. And ... maybe something unusual there.'

Zo wasn't sure she wasn't saying that to cheer her up.

'Where'd you get it?'

'I met some men fishing. This is strange, but in the bottom part of an old shopping centre. It's filled up with water and—'

'Oh, I've heard about that! What was it like?'

'Strange, beautiful. I was a little scared at first. Not that I didn't trust Ivar.'

'Ivar?'

'Someone from the house. Tall. A bit dodgy. But kind.' Zo wasn't sure how to describe Ivar. He was obviously up to no good. Surely part of a host of criminal activities. But she trusted him. There was something decent about him. Maybe that was wishful thinking. But she'd never felt afraid in his presence. He'd saved her after all. That night with the kids.

'Oh,' said Kyra, her disapproval or at least disinterest apparent.

'We came in through this back area. Dark and uncared for, and then it opened up. There was a lot of light streaming in from the skylights and the water made it magical.'

'They're just fish, Zo.'

'They asked me to sing,' she admitted, wondering now if they'd been teasing her.

'And did you?'

'I did,' said Zo, 'and then one of them gave me this tea.'

'I'd like to see it,' said Kyra. 'There's people doing really interesting stuff with hydroponic gardens and fish systems.' She bent over to scoop up the scattered remains of the banana and offer them to Beattie.

Zo wanted to offer to take her, but she wasn't sure it was the kind of place you could just show up. 'I could ask Ivar,' she said.

Kyra smiled. 'Maybe, if I'm brave. Beattie would love it.'

Those men wouldn't welcome a baby, Zo didn't think. She took a sip of her drink. It really was lovely. Soothing and lifting. But she couldn't taste anything special.

'Will you sing for me?' asked Kyra.

'Oh, no, I'm not a singer. It was just ... they wanted something. They seemed to want that.'

'But you're a musician.'

'I play the piano. I'll play you something sometime, though

you'd have to come to the house. It's not very portable.'

Kyra was looking at Beattie, cleaning her up. Very thoroughly, thought Zo, avoiding the question.

'That house,' said Kyra, 'it's a bit strange, isn't it? And the people?'

'They've all been really nice,' said Zo. Though that was not completely true. Kyra was right. It was strange. But what was wrong with a little strange?

Zo stood up and took all the makings to the sink. She washed up while Kyra took care of Beattie. 'Thank you,' she said when she'd finished. 'It was lovely to sit and chat for a bit.'

'Oh, but any time, Zo. And you came bearing gifts!'

She kissed Kyra on the cheek impulsively and let Beattie grab on to her finger. The rain had stopped, and when Zo left she turned to walk further up the street. She wasn't sure if she was ready to go back to the house yet. She wanted to walk it out, decide for herself.

The weather didn't settle. At times it was sunny. But at other times clouds threatened, although it never properly rained. Zo took her coat off, then put it back on again what seemed like a thousand times. An hour later she found herself at the cafe she'd waited in on the first day.

The barista had dyed his hair blue, or at least the bit of it poking out from the back of his beanie. He suggested hot chocolate and she agreed, more for the comfort than for the taste. 'How's your day been?' he asked. 'What have you been up to?'

'Just out walking,' said Zo. She never knew how to reply to those questions. She liked the man, but she didn't know what to say to him. She felt boring, inconsequential. Then, on impulse, she put her hand into her coat jacket and pulled out the packet of tea.

'What have you got?' he asked, eyes sparkling.

'Someone gave it to me. I wondered what it was.'

The man opened the packet carefully and held it up to his nose.

'Nice,' he said. 'Very nice.'

'Have some,' said Zo. She didn't want to lose it all, but how could she show him and not let him drink?'

'You don't mind?'

'No. I'd like you to try it.'

'I won't take it all.'

He handed Zo her hot chocolate and she left him. But by the time she had settled, he had joined her at the table, teapot and mug in hand. He handed the packet back to her, then spun the teapot around several times.

Zo watched him pour. The process seemed far more serious than it had at Kyra's house. Ceremonial and appreciative. He took a few slow sips.

'Can you tell what's in it?'

'Not sure,' he said. 'I think so. Cardamom, cloves, all the usual things. But something else.'

Zo waited, hoping, but the man shook his head. 'Can't place it. Can't be sure. It's good though.'

Zo smiled. She'd so hoped he could name the ingredient.

'Not everything has a name.'

He was like Kyra, thought Zo. Seeing her disappointment, trying to counter it.

'If we can recognise it, then we can name it,' she said.

'Can we?'

'Isn't that the way the brain is made? If we're capable of thinking it, we're capable of naming it.'

'Oh yes, thinking it. That's true. But not the recognising. Some things go on and we don't recognise them at all.'

'Flickering at the corner of your perception.'

'Doesn't mean they're not there.'

Another customer came in, and then another, and he was pulled away. She waved farewell as she left, but he was caught up at the coffee machine. Zo drifted out and into the world and succumbed to her longing to be back in her room at the top of the house.

Chapter Seven

Zo lay on her bed. She closed her eyes and imagined herself floating gently above her body. She listened to her heart flutter. It would rise, thump a few times, and then fall back. She tried to steady her breathing.

She wanted to free herself of her tangled thoughts. Nothing that had happened today had settled. Not that what had happened today was bad. She'd visited a friend and her gorgeous baby. She'd walked through the neighbourhood by the water. She'd sat in her favourite cafe and spoken with the barista. But nothing gelled. She knew it was because she'd wanted someone to find something fantastical in the tea. Something telling. But why? The tea had come from some old guys who'd found an out-of-the-way place to sit and fish. They weren't seers. They weren't anybody really. And they'd probably made her sing for a laugh. She blushed at the memory. She was a musician, she told herself. A faded, rusty, possibly never very good musician. But she had something. She could lose herself in the music. Sometimes she could even draw other people in.

With a burst of determination, she drew herself up from

the bed and across the room to the piano. The song of the other day had vanished. She'd thought she'd left it on the music rack, but it wasn't there, or in the piano stool. Zo stopped, paused, tried to recall the melody, tried to imagine something beautiful. But all she could think of was Debussy. She began the slow chords of *The Engulfed Cathedral*. At the edges of the sound, as each chord faded, she thought she could hear something else. Another tune, tinkling, livelier. But every time she stopped and took her hands off the keys, the other music disappeared. She began again, determined not to stop, but to keep listening at the edges. For a while she managed to hear the other tune at the corner. The music didn't fit well with hers. It wasn't trying to join in; it was trying to insinuate. A different piano, she thought, though one with a sharper, more jangling tone. Sometimes it seemed like a mandolin. But in the difficult middle section of her own piece she needed to concentrate, and it wasn't until the rumbles of the left hand stopped and she reached the final few bars that she heard it again. She played the chords as slowly and as quietly as she could, hoping that it didn't seem as if she was listening. And then, on the final chord, she held her fingers to the keys and the pedal to the floor until the very last echoes had faded to nothing.

The other music quickly dissipated. She caught the tail of sharp intervals and a jagged melodic line. But then it was gone. Probably it was Edda. Annoyed with her again. Trying to stop Zo playing. She laughed at the thought she could draw people in with her music. People were actively trying to fight her music off. But it soothed her, made her whole, if only while the song lasted.

She slid along the piano stool, meaning to return to the bed. Everything was dusty. The bed looked rusty and uninviting. The bedclothes were gone, leaving only a bedraggled mattress. The room itself was in disarray: the cornices were crumbling and there were lumps of plaster on the floor. Several of the floorboards, the ones closest to the window, were missing and the walls were faded and mouldy. She stood, pushing back the piano stool, and the room righted itself. The paint new, the bedclothes on the bed. Perhaps she was tired, away from home too long, and her imagination disquieted. She walked to the coat hanging on its hook, reached into the pocket, and felt for the packet of tea. Still there. No-one would steal it. It was only a packet of tea.

Zo sat on the bed and tried to push the vision of the decayed house out of her mind. She took her fly out of her bag. She could see messages there. Something from Michael, but the fly flickered and the messages fled. It was almost out of battery. She sat it on the solar mat close to the window and wondered that she could have neglected it so badly. She'd normally charge it every day.

The front door opened, and she heard heavy boots. Keys being flung. Callum was back! She smoothed down her clothes, looked at herself in the mirror and flung herself down the stairs, trying not to hurry. The foyer was empty, although there were no longer letters poking from Callum's mailbox. Were there footsteps? Breathing? She walked through to the lounge room at the back. No-one was sitting there; only Wirt's creations inhabited the space. But the door to another room was open. She steeled herself to walk to it, to look.

'Zo, is that you?'

She smiled, feigned surprise. 'Callum.'

'Sorry about the car.' He stood in the doorway, head almost to the lintel. He looked worn, as if he hadn't slept well for some time. Zo wondered, too late, what activities had warranted the extended use of her car. It could not matter now. It was back.

Zo tried to convey a nonchalance she didn't possess. Not that she cared about the car. But now that Callum was here, things seemed easier, more straightforward. 'You're back now.'

'Just for a moment. You don't need the car, do you?' asked Callum.

He still hadn't moved from the doorway, and Zo felt she couldn't move either. She was caught in the middle of the room. 'I guess not.'

'You sure?' Though he seemed sure enough. He wouldn't even have asked her if she hadn't come downstairs.

'How did it run?' she asked.

'Like a dream,' said Callum. Zo tilted her head. 'A noisy, uncomfortable dream. But she's solid. I knew I could depend on her.'

'We used to take her everywhere,' said Zo. She'd never referred to the campervan as she before. 'On holidays, lots of holidays. Some weekends we'd just throw some stuff in and go. The kids were younger then. Less complicated.'

'It smelled of the beach,' said Callum.

'Old fish,' said Zo.

'Happiness.'

Zo couldn't reply to that. For a moment she imagined Callum tossing her the keys, asking her to drive him somewhere. She knew it wasn't real, this thought, but it was real enough to catch her there, standing in the room.

'Sorry, Zo, I've got to get going.'

'Have fun.' Zo turned away and continued to the kitchen. Where she had never meant to go, but which now seemed her only haven. She waited there until she heard Callum leave, putting plates away, fussing around. She didn't want anything to eat or drink. She just wanted to hide. As soon as she heard the front door close, she ventured out. The door of Callum's study was closed but Zo tiptoed up to it, put her ear close to the wood and listened. There was no sound except for the groans and cracks of the house itself. She walked out into the foyer and up the stairs to her own room.

*

That night, after a subdued dinner where the other inhabitants of the house had been preoccupied with their own concerns, Zo retreated to bed and dreamed that she stood again in the dining room, turning as Callum spoke to her.

'Let me take you for a spin,' he said. And then he laughed. 'I mean, it's your van. You drive. But I want to show you something.'

'OK.' Callum tossed Zo the keys. She watched them as they rose into the air and down, wondering if she would catch them, but they landed cleanly in her hands. They walked out of the house together. The door opened without protest and the only wind was a playful one. The campervan was parked out the front by the gate.

'Where to?' asked Zo once they were inside the van, strapped in, ready to go.

'Watson's Bay.'

Zo was glad it was this side of the bridge. She'd thought he might say Manly, even Mosman. Somewhere close to home. It took a moment to remember how to persuade the campervan into action. It felt different, but cars always did when someone else had been driving them. By the time she turned the corner just past Kyra's house, Zo felt as if her old rational self had returned. She drove up over Anzac Bridge and then finally through to New South Head Road and out to the tip of Watson's Bay. She didn't need the GPS; she knew the way without thinking. She felt as if she could keep driving forever.

But then, in the dream, she parked the car on a narrow back road behind some shops. She followed Callum along the path to an old signal station. They were not the only people there, but with Callum Zo felt as if she was sheltered from the chatter and photos. The other people were scarcely real, transparent as if they were projections. And when they stood at the heads, looking at the ocean, it seemed to Zo that Callum was showing her a world which only he could reveal. One whale was clearly visible close to shore.

'That's a Southern Right,' Callum told her. 'And this morning there were Humpbacks, a little further out.' He said a lot more about whales, but Zo wasn't truly listening. Callum was standing behind her with one arm around her. She wanted him there, but she didn't lean into him. She had never felt like this before, outside the dream. But she realised now this was what she wanted. Did she? He passed her the binoculars, and she took them obediently. She didn't feel the need to see the whales up close. It was enough that they were there. But she took them and put the binoculars up to her eyes, adjusted as best she could.

'Oh,' she said, when she'd found them. Despite herself.

'Beautiful, huh.' And he pulled her closer towards him as if she was a whale too. As if her blubber and barnacles were the very things that drew him to her. Zo hadn't expected this closeness when she'd agreed to the drive earlier. But she didn't resist it now. It seemed part of her fate. Part of the sun and the waves and the grass. It was what she had been looking for.

Afterwards, they walked down to the bay and ate fish and chips from a wooden kiosk perched over the water. Water lapped over what used to be a walkway, but a narrow bridge had been built so that the cafe was still accessible. Some people kayaked out, grabbing what seemed to be preordered food as they swept past. The wooden structure of the cafe looked precarious and vulnerable. It could not be long before it entirely succumbed to the waves.

They walked back over the footbridge and sat on the sloping grass to eat their food. Seagulls came close enough to catch any crumbs, but not yet so close that Zo felt overwhelmed. She could see the towers of the city in the distance across the water. Callum seemed further away now. He was not the man who had held her close to him as they'd looked out over the ocean.

She should drive home now. Drop Callum off and keep going in one great loop back to her real house. Her fly was there, charging. She didn't really need it. The dream seemed to be pulling her to the car, but she kept thinking of the house, of going back to the room. That was where her things were. And Callum. That was where he lived. She didn't want to be with him. She was half-awake now, but she kept diving back in, trying to get the dream to turn out right. She didn't know what she wanted. There were times she thought she knew, but inside the dream she couldn't pull the right way. And when she finally woke up, she couldn't remember how she had wanted it to end.

Chapter Eight

Zo didn't want to walk any closer to the machines, but there was no other choice if she was to make it to the shops. She stopped outside Kyra's garden, willing herself to go further. There were markers on the road opposite Kyra's gate, though she could make no sense of them. The noise was overwhelming. A voice floated above the clamour: Kyra stood by her front door, arms waving, mouth grinning. Zo hesitated, but the machines started another round of unholy music, so she opened the gate and fled up Kyra's path, through the vines and bushes to the door.

Kyra ushered her in, anxious to slam the door behind them. They went through to the back to an enclosed veranda. It was the kind of space that Zo might once have longed to rip open, but now it was a haven, the glass another padding against the noise.

'Sit,' said Kyra before she disappeared.

Zo found a cane chair covered in several layers of cushions and sat, exhausted, as if she'd been running all morning.

Kyra brought her tea. Something herbal, something from the garden Zo guessed, and she made appreciative noises.

'What are they doing?'

'It's solar coating for the road. It's a good thing, really. More green power, less heat from the road.'

'What about your garden?'

'It'll survive.'

'Wirt will hate it.'

Kyra tilted her head. 'They're not going as far as that house.'

'Oh.' The house was just down the road, but there was a look on Kyra's face that told Zo not to ask, that Kyra didn't want to explain.

There was a rapping sound from the front, and a voice calling for entry. 'Stay,' said Kyra. She ran up to open the door.

The corridor filled with wails and excited exchanges. All of which stopped as soon as they saw Zo. She was an interloper.

'I should go.'

'No, no, please stay,' said Kyra. 'At least till they're done outside.'

'Don't mind us.' A buxom woman covered in turquoise swept past her and into a chair. 'I'm Hatty.' She held out a hand covered in rings.

'Zo.' Zo stretched forward, grasped the hand. It was soft and warm.

'Zo's staying down the road.'

The group rustled. They all found perches, enveloping Zo. Some were less certain of her than others, but they were all curious.

'You were at the Moses day,' said one. She seemed younger than the rest. And Zo only realised now that there was a baby asleep in a cloth covered box at her feet.

'Usually we work in the garden,' said Hatty.

'But not today,' said Kyra. She had produced more tea and

tiny cakes dripping with syrup.

They were all too beautifully dressed to work in a garden. And Hatty's rings, Zo couldn't see them being willingly covered in dirt.

Instead, they told her stories of the garden's beginnings. How they had found each other and come together. What hard work it had been, in the beginning, how they thought Kyra was crazy to plant in her front garden and on the verge. And how they'd been right! People had stolen things. Not just the poor or the needy, but rich people, pulling up in expensive cars to snatch herbs. Basil, they were mad for basil! As if they couldn't grow it themselves. The herbs were in tubs now, out the back.

'If people want to take, that's fine,' said Kyra. 'It is all a gift from the earth to us all.'

Zo sensed a shift of raised eyebrows and disagreement, but these women knew each other well. They knew how to compromise and tolerate; they probably knew how to get their own way when it was something important.

Hatty told a story, obviously told many times before, of the way in which they'd discovered a thief. 'Bold as you like, pure cheek, in broad daylight.' And how she'd grabbed him from behind and one of the other women, Gadah, had approached the thief holding out a fiercely pronged garden fork and together the two women had seen him off.

'It wasn't that bad!' Gadah said.

'Oh, you would have poked him,' said one of the other women.

'Filled him full of holes.'

'Peeing six ways at once!'

The laughter burst from all the women, and even Kyra was

smiling, though Zo thought that she would have let the thief go with a load of herbs and vegetables in his hands.

Zo listened to them chatter until, finally, she realised the noise from the road had died down. She said her farewells, sad to be leaving, but understanding that she was not part of it. It was her arms that Kyra loaded up with vegetables this time, and Zo felt a little like the rich thief, taking so much home.

*

Zo stood in the kitchen. She'd abandoned the idea of going to the shops and had returned home. She found the percolator, found the coffee, but was startled by the creak of the kitchen door. Zo had never seen it opened. She was relieved to see it was only Edda coming in from a back garden Zo hadn't even realised was there. The other woman had gathered something green, herbs most likely, and she seemed content, although when she saw Zo, her face turned back in on itself. She plonked the herbs down on the bench and ran the water in the kitchen sink. So much water, thought Zo, so wasteful, although the city was hardly in drought. Edda poured dishwashing liquid over her fingers and rubbed them together, meticulously ridding herself of some invisible dirt. Something about the action repelled Zo. She was mesmerised by it, thinking all the while: I would never do that. But what was wrong with it? It seemed unhygienic, though Zo could not have articulated exactly why. It seemed wrong.

'Are you making coffee?' asked Edda. Her voice so startled Zo that she spilt the packet of coffee grounds she'd been holding. She scooped them up, then hesitated, not knowing if Edda would be offended if she used them to make coffee, fearing she would think her wasteful if she threw them out.

'Use them,' said Edda, and Zo trickled them into the percolator. She fiddled with the stove, trying to bring herself under control.

She turned to see Edda drawing in the escaped coffee grounds. Her finger traced a stick figure and then a sun. A child's picture. 'We used to paint with coffee,' she said. 'Sad, brown pictures. That was all there was.' She erased the drawing with her palm and then carefully scooped up the last of the spilt grounds and tipped them into a plastic bucket. 'For the worms,' she said.

'I never knew there was a garden,' said Zo.

'Not much,' said Edda. 'Pots, mostly.' She reached up to scoop her hair back and Zo saw the scars along the inside of both forearms. Edda caught her staring and stood, arms up, showing the scars, daring Zo to comment.

'What happened?' asked Zo. It was too personal a question, she knew, but she wanted to prove she wasn't scared to ask.

'We are more or less the same age,' said Edda. Zo nodded and Edda released her arms from their display. 'When you were a little girl,' continued Edda, 'you were happy, I expect. Safe. Loved.' Edda couldn't know if Zo's childhood had been happy or unhappy. But now did not seem to be the time to object. 'I was locked away. Behind bars. Not for a crime.' And the word crime carried more bitterness than any word Zo had ever heard.

'You were a refugee,' guessed Zo.

Edda inclined her head. It was half a nod. An acquiesce rather than an agreement.

'I wanted someone to come down and scoop me up,' she said. 'I would have left my parents and flown away. They disintegrated. They dissolved. They left me there alone.'

'I'm sorry,' said Zo.

Edda raised her eyebrows, tilted her head away. 'But it wasn't your fault,' she said. Although she clearly felt it was, in some inexplicable way, Zo's fault.

'Is that where you met Reuben?'

'No. Reuben came later. Reuben knows how to hope.' There was a pause. Zo could see Edda regretted the words. 'Why do you stay?' asked Edda. 'Doesn't your family miss you?'

'They're away at the moment.'

'And your friends, your house?'

The air shifted a little then, the kitchen closing in on them. 'I guess I felt like a break.'

'So, any moment now, you'll go back home.'

'Of course,' said Zo. But she wondered how that could be true. Her time here seemed to stretch out as if she were the one behind some invisible bars, longing for something to take her away. Callum still had her car, but even that seemed insubstantial now. To even mention it seemed foolish.

'You need to offer the heart,' said Edda. Although Zo must have misheard her. But Edda had taken her coffee and had walked out of the kitchen to the back garden. Zo took her own cup to the couch in the lounge near the back window. Even with the curtains pulled back, the backyard was difficult to see. The trees belonged to other houses, Zo thought. They were too far away. There was grass and some old pavers and a crumbling chair. But no Edda. And no real garden. Not even a small one with pots.

Chapter Nine

'I have to get out.' It burst out of Zo, unexpected. Plain and true.

'You don't say.' Ivar was at the mailboxes. Listening, but not turning towards her. 'There's something it wants from you,' he said as if reading the contents of the next envelope.

'It?' Though Zo knew, really, what the it was. It was this house. It had given her the piano, taken her car, tried to entice her.

Ivar shook his head. He beckoned her with two fingers, still turned away from her. He headed into the lounge room and turned to the right, sidling along the wall as if he wanted to look more closely at Wirt's creations. He paused, still facing into the room, reached back and opened the door to the study. The door where Zo had last seen Callum. He turned his head towards her, put a finger to his lips.

'I'll make the coffee,' he said. 'Want to show you how to wrestle that percolator.'

Zo opened her mouth to protest, but Ivar shook his head again. He walked towards the kitchen, deliberately not looking back, it seemed to Zo.

She could feel her heart beating fast. She could keep going, follow Ivar into the kitchen, or sit at the table and wait for him. Everything could go on as before. Except that it couldn't. She took the two steps to the open door, looked into the study. There was enough light coming in through the windows for her to see cobwebs and the layer of dust that covered the floor, the desk, the cracked swivel chair. It was an old house, thought Zo, and Callum hadn't been here for a while. Then she was in, crossing the room, right up to the desk. A mountain of mail, more mail than one person could possibly accumulate in a few weeks. She saw the kind of names she'd half expected: Earthwatch Institute, Ocean Defender, Cetacean Study. Down at the bottom of the pile, the envelopes were yellowed and dirty. Some had been chewed by cockroaches or other bugs. Callum wasn't a man who would be overly ordered, thought Zo. But there were bills there too. Bills with red writing visible through the window. She left them; it was wrong of her to look. These were Callum's concerns, not hers.

The wall above the desk was covered in photos. Most stuck on with tacks or sticky tape, but one in a frame, showing Callum standing beside a ship with huge red shark teeth painted on the bow. Callum was grinning. He looked almost the same age as he was now. The other photos looked as if they had been taken out at sea, on board the same ship. A few of dolphins, one of a whale, most of them other crew members. They looked tired, happy, ragged.

And then, on the desk, an open envelope, a council letter. Forced demolition, rising water, unfit for habitation. The room fizzed around her. It was solid enough, this place. Only in need of some care and attention. But this room, so neglected,

Callum couldn't possibly be —Clangs from the kitchen and loud swearing from Ivar brought her out of her thoughts. She stepped out of the room as quickly as she could, closing the door behind her.

'Shit, Zo, there's no coffee, don't know who the fuck has drunk it all.'

'I'll shout you one,' said Zo.

Ivar looked at her closely. 'You're on,' he said.

'I need my bag,' said Zo.

'Bloody hurry,' said Ivar, and he whisked her away with his fingers.

He was standing with the front door open when Zo came back down the stairs. She couldn't help but run through the doorway and down the path a little.

'You don't have to run all the way to the shops,' said Ivar once she was through the gate.

'How ...'

But Ivar shook his head and they walked in silence. Zo paused at the doorway of her usual haunt. She worried that the barista might be part of the artifice, but Ivar looked happy enough to go inside.

'This your regular?' he asked.

Zo nodded and they walked in. The barista greeted her, though he looked warily at Ivar. Ivar chose a table in the corner and Zo sat, stunned. Neither of them spoke until the drinks arrived. Zo couldn't think of what to say, how to start. She didn't want it confirmed.

'Now do you understand?' asked Ivar at last.

'No! Not at all. I don't understand. I don't understand how you can live there. I don't understand how I met him when he's ...' Zo couldn't say it.

'Dead, Zo. Dead. The man doesn't exist anymore.'

'I met him. He showed me to my room. We all had dinner.' You were there, she thought.

'Part of her charm,' said Ivar.

'Her?'

'Do I have to spell it out?'

'Yes,' said Zo. 'Yes, you do.'

'It's the house. Surely you've figured that out. The house wants you to stay. It wants something from you. It's manipulating things so that you do.'

'It's a house.'

'It's old, Zo. Old and wily. Maybe it's gathered up enough time to have evolved into something more.'

'And you can live there knowing that?'

'So you believe me?'

'Yes,' whispered Zo, though she looked at her coffee when she said it.

'She doesn't hurt me; I don't hurt her.'

'And the others?'

'Wirt's already mad. Got no idea if he knows or cares. Tim can't see what's right under his nose. Reuben? Yeah, I think Reuben's figured it out. Which means Edda has at least heard his theories, but Edda ...' Ivar spread his hands.

'She seems so connected to reality.'

'Ha!'

'I mean she's so aware of what she's been through, how the world is.'

'And I'm not?'

Zo didn't know Ivar well enough to reply. But he wasn't

the wounded, bitter spirit that Edda was. He seemed to be fundamentally at peace with whatever life had dealt him.

'Look, it's only a theory,' he said after a moment.

'And what about Callum; you're telling me he's a ghost.'

'Maybe not a ghost. Maybe an echo. You've never spoken with him outside of the house, have you.'

'No,' said Zo. She thought of her dream and the thought made her shudder. It had seemed so real, so true. Now it was just someone playing tricks on her. 'And my car?'

Ivar's face was a complicated mix of amusement and regret. 'You want me to show it to you?'

'You took it.'

Ivar feigned shock. 'Nup, not me.'

'No more walking,' said Zo. 'Just tell me.'

'It's still at the garage.'

'But I got a call!'

'Yeah, you got a call, they said it was ready, and then?'

'Then Callum went and got it.'

'So you told the garage there was someone else who would come and pick it up?'

Zo shook her head. 'They've not called me back.'

'You paid for it?'

'I paid over the phone.'

'You're going to have to come on this walk with me, then.'

Zo stirred the bottom of her coffee and dredged up the foam and sugar with her spoon. She would walk with Ivar to see her car. And then what? She would go home. There would be no reason to stay. Why did she want to? She was mad, possessed. A feeling of nausea crept up on her. Why would she want to stay in a derelict house with a ghostly owner? A house that might never let her go if she walked back inside again.

'I found the brochure here,' she said.

'Of course you did.'

Zo looked around, trying to find the stand she'd seen the first day. There were newspapers in one corner, a few business cards pinned to a corkboard. The brochure had been on her table, she was sure. She'd picked it up without thinking, without moving from her seat. 'Can I leave?'

'Will she let you? I don't know.' Ivar put his mug down, looked at Zo straight and blunt. 'But you don't even want to try, do you?'

'I do,' said Zo. 'I do, it's just that ...'

'You don't want to.'

She tilted her head to one side. The barista was watching them closely. She'd liked him, shown him the tea. But he'd known too, all along.

'One of those men you took me to see told me to stay.'

Ivar laughed. 'Those crazy dudes. All they care about is fish and having a chat. Mostly tall stories. Plus their English ... not so good.'

But Ivar hadn't treated them like this when he'd taken her to see the fish. He hadn't laughed at them then.

'Look, Zo, we'll go get your car, then you can make your choice. Doesn't mean you have to drive away in it today. Just means you could.'

'Why are you doing this?' asked Zo.

'Maybe I think she made a mistake.' Ivar got up and left so that Zo couldn't see his face. But she felt as if he had slapped her. Who was she, after all, to live here and have a favourite coffee shop, make friends with a next-door neighbour? Edda would be glad to see Zo go. Wirt and Reuben would forget she'd even been there.

Zo followed Ivar out of the shop as quickly as she could. Ivar had started off down the footpath, turning north towards the garage.

'What about Tim?' she asked.

'What about him?'

'Is he trapped too?'

'I'm hurt, Zo. You're totally fine with me living in a haunted mansion, but Tim, the one who loves such stuff, him you're worried about.'

'You said you had an arrangement. Besides, you're an adult.'

'Strictly speaking Tim's an adult too.'

'No, he's not.'

It took them ten minutes to reach the garage. A ten-minute journey Zo could have made any day, easily, if only she'd had thought to walk it. There was the campervan, parked in one forlorn corner, looking dirty and weathered.

Zo saw the men in the shaded workshop. She didn't want to speak to them. She'd paid. That was enough. Usually, the keys were under the windshield. She headed to her car, but a large figure lumbered out of the workshop, rag in hand, a strange look on his face. Zo saw the nod he gave to Ivar, wondered what that connection implied.

'Thought you'd forgotten us,' the mechanic joked.

'I'm sorry,' said Zo. 'There was a misunderstanding. A friend of mine ...'

'Should charge you for parking.'

'Of course,' said Zo. 'I'm so sorry.' She reached into her bag.

'Nup, don't worry about it,' the mechanic said. His tone was slightly disappointed. Zo was sure that something had passed between him and Ivar while she'd been searching for her wallet. 'Anyway, it's all good. She's running well, as well as can be expected for something of this vintage.' He patted the campervan, gave it his approval for the road.

Ivar reached for the passenger's side door, hopped in and released Zo from the man's attention.

'Thank you,' said Zo.

'Keys are under the windshield,' he said as he turned and walked away.

Zo got in, found the keys, started the car. She always felt self-conscious driving at the garage, as if her technique had been the reason the car had been there in the first place. But she manoeuvred the car out of its space and over the concrete courtyard, ready to turn into the street.

'Where to?' asked Ivar.

'I'll take you home.' Zo couldn't look at him.

'On your own head.' He didn't try and stop her.

The drive took less than five minutes. Not long enough to make a choice. Zo parked the campervan close to the front gate where she could see it, her means of freedom.

'I want to play the piano one last time,' she said.

'Of course.' They climbed out of the car together, Ivar holding the gate open for her. Sarcastically, thought Zo, but she went up to the turquoise door, touched the whale's tail knocker and walked in, trying not to think about lost protectors of the ocean.

Chapter Ten

Zo's room seemed newly shabby. Just the shadow of Ivar's story, she tried to tell herself. It seemed incredible, now that she was by herself, although she could not deny the fact of the van. Callum, wherever he was, did not have it. She sat on the bed and the thought of her own house was a sudden urgent longing. There was no need to stay here. The girls would return from camp soon. Michael would start making noises then. Why hadn't he protested more? He was still away, of course. Preoccupied with work, as he always was on overseas trips. She dug through her bag for her fly, saw that there were messages waiting, though she didn't have the heart to look at them. Instead, she opened the wing, found pictures of the house, of the girls, even one of Michael. There was a video the girls had made when they were younger, full of giggles and then a ridiculous dance that was more about them than about her but at the end they'd jumped up, yelling, 'Happy Birthday!' And, as they came back down, 'Love you, Mum.'

The thought of that dusty room downstairs with the pile of mail and the ominous letters on the desk crept up on her. Zo's own study was a place of retreat. The old chair she'd taken an age to choose, the lamp with the circus patterns which danced around the room when it was on. Her home had seemed cold and suburban when she was first here. But now she wondered why she'd abandoned it so easily. This was not the place she belonged.

But the piano called to her. That was the heart of it, finding the piano here. She'd felt recognised, chosen in some way. A mistake, Ivar had said. She'd not been brave enough to ask him why. As if it was some bourgeois failing of hers which made Ivar want to release her.

She opened the piano, played the first chords of *The Engulfed Cathedral*. She let herself become lost in the music. While she played, she didn't have to think, she didn't have to decide. And this was the best person she was, even if it was not enough. As the piece built up its crash of sound, she found herself angry. Partly at being tricked into staying, but mostly because she had now been rejected. And she was angry at the tears that formed while her left hand rippled away. She let the music build. Why had she given this up? Why hadn't she persevered? Become better, more sure. Made a career.

She stood, found the fly, looked at her messages. The girls would be back in three days, Michael was worried about her, but he was in Singapore for the next week. 'I hope we'll see you when I return,' were his words. As if she'd abandoned him. She rang, but of course he wasn't there. Zo wasn't sure of the time difference, but he would be either asleep or engrossed by work. Three days, then. She would give it three days. Discover what it was she had been called here to do, mistake or no. And in three days' time she would go. Back to her own family. She texted the girls. Perhaps they'd get it; maybe they weren't allowed phones or flies on camp. She couldn't remember.

She closed the door to her room, walked down one flight and knocked on Ivar's door before she had time to stop herself. The door to Wirt's room was open and she saw him standing, fiddling with what looked to be a giant moth. She waited, heart beating, trying to hold on to the angry propulsion that had pushed her down the stairs. Trying not to let her foolishness speak too strongly in her mind. Ivar finally opened the door.

'What needs to be done?' asked Zo.

'Depends. Whose side are you on?'

'There are sides?'

'Course there are.'

'I could find out who owns the house now, or who has jurisdiction, stop it being torn down, get some repairs ...'

Ivar shook his head. 'It's not that kind of problem. Besides, Reuben's working on that right now. He has that kind of careful mind.'

Zo was annoyed at both the implication she didn't have the right kind of mind and that she'd suggested something mundane. 'What kind of problem is it then?'

'Sorrow,' said Ivar.

'A life that hasn't found itself yet,' added Wirt. He'd come out of his room and was now standing on the landing not far behind Zo. She turned to him. He was holding the moth balanced on one arm and it seemed like an old-fashioned version of her dragonfly.

'Yearning,' she said.

Both men nodded.

'What can be done about that?' We are all yearning, she thought, though mostly we cover it up. Life is yearning for something that can never quite be touched.

'We need to go into the basement,' said Wirt.

'Nothing there,' said Ivar.

Zo realised this was an old conversation. 'What does Tim think?'.

'Tim doesn't understand,' said Ivar.

'Are you sure?'

'How can he?' asked Ivar. He'd come out of his room and was propelling Zo by the elbow down the stairs. Wirt followed them, but slowly and at a distance. Ivar took her down only one flight. Tim's door was ajar, but he wasn't there. Zo could hear faint voices coming from Reuben's room, and Zo thought perhaps she was to be offered to Reuben as a helper, but Ivar led her to another closed door.

'This is Callum's room,' he said.

Zo turned to the two men.

'You need to go in if you want to understand,' said Wirt.

Just another room, thought Zo. Though even Ivar seemed reluctant to touch the door.

'I don't know what it is you expect me to do,' she said.

'That song you keep playing,' said Ivar, 'what's it called?'

'*The Engulfed Cathedral.* Debussy,' she said. She'd told him that before.

'Drowned,' said Wirt.

'But it would rise up,' said Zo. 'Out of the waves, out of the fog,'

'And was it rescued?' asked Wirt.

'No,' said Zo, 'it sinks down again.'

'Perhaps she wants to rise up and stay up,' suggested Wirt.

Zo looked at Ivar, hoping for a more practical interpretation.

But he was looking straight at her. Daring her to do something.

Zo grabbed the doorknob and opened the door. She took two steps inside the room before she could stop herself. She didn't look back, although she could feel Ivar and Wirt's eyes on her, hear Edda's laugh from somewhere else in the house. It was ordinary, this room. Clean, tidy, uncluttered. A made bed, a small table beside it with only a clock on it. A white wooden chest of drawers, clear of any ornamentation. There were no pictures on the walls. The window was closed, but the curtains were open. No dust. Bare wooden boards, polished some time ago but clean. A rug with faded geometric patterns in navy and cream. It could have been a showcase room if the furniture were newer. There were no personal touches.

Zo looked back at the two men. There was nothing remarkable here. They were still in the corridor, though to Zo they seemed as if they were further away. They watched her, silent and wary. She shrugged her shoulders, trying to convey that this was an empty room.

She turned back, hoping to offer them some unassailable evidence of normality, even persuade them to come into the room themselves, but now there was a man sitting on the end of the bed. Callum.

'Zo.' Callum stretched out a hand to her as if this assignation had already been arranged.

Zo shook her head, took a step back. She stretched one arm back, wanting the solidity of the door frame, but she couldn't reach. Edda laughed again. Edda, who never laughed. They must all know, but what could they expect her to do?

'I got the car from the garage,' she said.

Callum nodded. She felt as if she was telling Michael

her boring domestic tales at the end of the day. Things that needed to be known, but that didn't really matter.

'I ... I don't understand who you are.'

'We've already met, Zo.'

'Are you a ghost?'

'Do I look like a ghost?'

'Then walk out of this room with me. Come for a drive in the car. Prove to me you're real.'

'Not now, Zo. I'm needed here.'

'You told me you were hardly ever here, that you were always out at sea, defending the whales.'

'The whales,' said Callum. He paused for a moment, as if he was trying to retrieve a memory. 'They're all gone now.'

'That's not true. You took me to see some ...' But that had been a dream.

'I've done all I can,' said Callum.

'And now?'

'Now, my job is here.'

He looked real, thought Zo. Corporeal, substantial. She wanted to touch him, to prove he wasn't an illusion. She tried to remember if she ever had. He'd held her hand, stopped her throwing Tim's dice. He'd seemed real then.

'Three clouds,' she told him. 'On the dice, three rain clouds.'

'I know,' said Callum. 'I warned you.'

'But what does that mean?'

'You can't hold back water,' he said. 'No matter what you do, it finds a way in.'

'What can I do?' she asked, understanding nothing.

'Learn how to float,' he said. He held out his hand again.

This time Zo stepped forward to take it. He seemed less troublesome now, more a man in need of saving. Perhaps he was just shy, a hermit who wanted to learn how to come back to life. Perhaps he was no more a ghost than she was.

She took a step over the clear, clean boards. One foot touched the edge of the rug.

'Did you drink the tea?' he asked.

'Yes,' said Zo. How did Callum know about the shopping centre fishermen? She moved towards him and took his hand. And as she did so, she felt herself falling through the house, through the rotten boards and the crumbling plaster, through the decayed carpet, the mouse droppings and the cockroaches, through to the soft earth at the bottom of the house.

Chapter Eleven

Zo felt as if she was still falling, but really she was lying in the mud. She felt it through her hair, seeping into her clothes and shoes. All she could see were clouds. Grey clouds sinking low and threatening rain once more. There was a bare tree over to the right. A shaft of light at just the right angle found spiderwebs – perfect circles suspended between the winter branches. It was beautiful and she knew if she shifted, it would be gone.

She heard a voice, faintly, as if from several feet away, but when she turned she saw boots. Tim's boots, she thought, and she sat up and grasped the hand that had reached down to her. It took her a moment to get her bearings. She was dizzy and incomplete. Her back ached.

'Are you alright?' he asked. Distant, wary.

'Tim, it's me, Zo.' The boy's face looked puzzled. As if he'd done enough to help a person in need without them claiming an association with him. It was Tim, she was sure it was. Zo wiped herself down, hoping to get the worst of the mud off. She gathered her hair and pushed it behind her. 'You know,' she said, 'from the house.'

'What house?' he asked, and Zo saw that the house was gone. That she was standing in the place the house used to be.

'You had the dice,' continued Zo. She knew it sounded desperate, but she couldn't stop herself. 'I came up with three clouds. And the cards, the woman with her feet in the water.'

A flash of something that might be recognition moved across Tim's face, but then he looked down at their feet. It had begun to drizzle. Light, warm, comforting drops, but already the mud was turning into pools. 'Is that your car?' asked Tim. 'Only it's not safe to park there, that's why I came in.' He was hoping, Zo saw, that she was somebody ordinary. Someone who'd probably slipped and knocked her head but who would come back to herself and stop troubling him.

'Show me,' said Zo.

Tim led her out to the street. There was the campervan, right on the street, close to the front gate where she'd parked it. It looked dirty, almost mouldy, as if it had been standing out in the weather for some time. There was a cluster of tickets under the windscreen wipers. Fines, though most were so faded that they were illegible. Zo grabbed them and opened the passenger door. It never locked. There, on the seat, were her keys, guarded by an enormous moth. Its brown wings were patterned like rippled bark, and it had a dark shiny body with yellow stripes. It could have been one of Wirt's. As soon as the door opened it rose into the air and flew towards Zo, landing on her shoulder in just the way her dragonfly would.

'You have a moth,' said Tim.

Zo would have liked to have brushed it off, but she didn't want to hurt it. 'Can I give you a lift?' she asked.

Tim shook his head. 'Do you think it's cruel?' he asked.

'Do I think what's cruel?'

'The moths, you know, the way they implant them when they're pupae. It's not meant to hurt. But ...'

'The moths?'

'I guess you think it's OK since you have one.'

'This moth isn't mine,' said Zo.

'You sure?' asked Tim. His face was wary. He was doubting her sanity all over again. 'Put out your hand.'

Zo held her hand out, open palm, and the moth immediately flew to it, landing on her palm. As far as she could tell it was a living, breathing creature, fuzzy and shaking. Up close like this, her dragonfly was completely still, and the plastics of its components were obvious. But that was necessary. When you took off a wing to use as a screen, or when you took it apart, or even plugged it in, you didn't want to feel as if you were handling a living thing.

'I guess it is mine,' she said. She wanted to ask how this moth was different from a fly, what this moth could and couldn't do. But she didn't want him to think her stranger than he already did.

'You said you saw the queen,' Tim said.

'The queen of clubs. Standing in the water.' Tim was quiet, watchful. 'You showed me a card trick,' Zo continued. 'Ordinary cards, then they turned into something extraordinary. And I choose the queen.' She saw the look on Tim's face. 'Maybe I'm wrong. I thought I recognised you. I'm sorry.'

Tim shook his head. 'I don't use those cards.' He looked down. One of his boots was scuffing at the footpath. 'Can I show you something?'

'Sure,' said Zo. She took the keys out of the car and closed the door. The moth flew up to her shoulder and settled there. She followed Tim, but a few steps down the street, she looked back at the empty lot. No sign of the house, only mud and weeds. Even the front stairs were gone. She looked to see if she could see anything she recognised in the street, but they had already gone too far; the street had dipped too low to tell.

At the bottom of the road, the water lapped so high that it had overtaken the stone walls. The water was right on the road, so that a vehicle might find itself driving out into the bay with nothing to stop it. There wasn't even a temporary barrier. Zo remembered the solar road coating and the way in which they had abandoned their project outside Kyra's house. They had known this was inevitable. Zo's feet were close to the foamy water.

'It's come up so far,' said Zo.

'This is low. I told you, the car isn't safe there.'

'I'll move it soon.'

Tim was silent, looking at something to their left, down on a stretch of muddy rocks. A group of men had gathered. Officials, dressed in high-visibility gear with strong boots and an air of purpose. And then she saw the body: limp, waterlogged, bedraggled.

'Usually, they're swept away,' said Tim, 'but this one never made it.'

'Never made it where?'

Tim kept looking out at the water. Zo felt that he was deliberately not facing her.

'They think that the water can carry them to something better.'

'But not you.'

'Maybe,' said Tim.

'Don't,' said Zo.

'What else is there?'

'That person down there on the rocks isn't some place better.'

'But only because he didn't succeed.'

Zo placed a hand on Tim's arm, but then took it away. He was so cold, so wet, so unmoved. She didn't know what she could offer him.

'It rains all the time,' he said. 'There's nothing but water and ... this world isn't built for it. Maybe it's better to dive in, be wholly part of something.'

'You can only be wholly part of something if you can survive,' said Zo.

'How do you know?'

Zo had nothing to say to that. Memories bubbled up: a younger self being caught by what seemed like huge waves, of being dragged along the sharp ocean floor, of thinking she would never breathe again. Memories of desperately trying to swim to shore against a tide that seemed determined to sweep her out.

'You know,' she said at last. 'Don't do it.'

Tim turned, sharp, alive, fierce. 'Of course I won't.'

They watched as the men made their way across the rocks towards an old set of concrete stairs. The body had been covered and placed on a stretcher. It was slow going with a heavy, awkward burden and the rocks uneven and slippery with mould. All this time the drizzle had kept on, so that Zo could see a mist of drops covering Tim's hair and arms.

'Let me drop you somewhere,' she said.

Tim nodded and began to walk up the road. Zo wasn't sure if it was an agreement. The old Tim, the Tim that she knew, shared the same desperate sadness. This one seemed almost entirely without hope. She was glad when he slid into the passenger's seat of her car. She dropped her bag in the back, said a silent prayer. The campervan started immediately with a strong kick of petrol and power.

'I feel like I'm about to go on holiday,' said Tim.

Zo looked over at him. 'Where would you like to go?'

His face closed again. 'I'm staying with friends. Just up the road.'

The van took its time ascending the hill. Zo turned to see if Kyra's house seemed intact. The garden seemed as fertile as ever, though Zo thought she spotted extra canopies over sections of the front yard.

'There used to be a community garden in that house,' she said.

'Still is,' said Tim. 'Run by some group of women.'

'They were nice,' said Zo.

'Maybe.'

She followed his directions, through narrow side streets and back ways, but always up, always higher. None of the houses looked well cared for.

'Just here,' said Tim. Zo pulled over as best she could. There was a man standing in the open front door. He had a large knife in his hand which he appeared to be using to peel vibrantly coloured fruit.

'Ivar,' said Zo.

'You know him?'

Zo made a noncommittal shrug. She'd thought she'd

known Tim. She did know Tim, but Tim did not know her. 'He lives with you?'

'Sometimes,' said Tim. 'You can come in if you like.'

Zo was tempted. But she'd intruded on enough lives. And she was covered in mud and dishevelled. 'Another time,' she said. The man who may have been Ivar greeted Tim and waved at her with his knife. It was a friendly enough gesture, though not so friendly as to make her change her mind. She watched until both men were inside and the door was shut, then she pulled out from the kerb and made her way back out to the main street. She didn't try to programme the GPS. The moth had taken up residency on the front dashboard, just out of reach.

Zo manoeuvred through what traffic there was. There weren't many people out. Delivery vans, a lot of motorbikes, but she couldn't see any other cars like hers, driven by a person out and about for their own personal concerns. She turned easily onto the road she knew would take her over the bay and home the long way around. It was usually a difficult turn, but even here there was hardly any traffic. Up on the first bridge she felt alone and exposed, as if she and the campervan were the only things left in the world. A group of white birds wheeled just ahead of her, heedless of the van. Zo slowed, more for her sake than theirs. They were smart enough and fast enough to get out of the way. She turned the radio on, found static at first, flicked through the presets. She caught the end of a dramatic orchestral piece, with a storm of voices filling the last chords. She couldn't place it, but it didn't niggle at her; she was using the music to fill up the emptiness of the world. And then, coming out of the speakers, was Debussy.

Girl with the Flaxen Hair, from the same book of preludes as *The Engulfed Cathedral*.

It felt almost as if she was playing the piece herself. She pulled to the side of the road but kept the ignition on and let the Debussy continue. Three days, she remembered. She'd given herself three days. And already she was heading home. A wallaby bounded out in front of her, crossing the road in one brown spurt. Although there was no need; it could have taken its time. It could have wandered out, the way the bush turkeys did at home, and nothing would have hit it. Zo wiped away her tears. The thought that this road would take her anywhere seemed foolish now. She seemed to be heading further into bushland, away from people. Sydney was like that. Pockets of bush interspersed with houses. Fingers of harbour finding their way between factories and warehouses. But you never felt as if you had lost the city. There were always enough people, enough lights, enough signs that the bush was being held back. But here? Zo wasn't sure that there would be anyone at home to find. She wasn't sure that the would be a home to head to. It would be too final to find out for sure. And she had promised three days.

The Debussy ended. The sound of an announcer's voice filtered through to her. Somewhere there were people. She wasn't lost in the bush. She ran the wipers twice over the windscreen, turned the car around and headed back over the bridge. A Sculthorpe clarinet pierced the air with its lonely yearning. Zo had no idea what she would do now. She would find Ivar. He'd got her into this, him and Wirt, but what use was Wirt? At least she knew where Ivar was.

Chapter Twelve

It was easy enough to find the shops, but it took some time for Zo to find the house where she had dropped Tim. Even now, standing by the front step, she wasn't completely sure. There were dead plants in pots on the small porch, but a vine was encroaching on the porch railing. The front door was a faded red. She tried to remember it from before, but all she had really noticed was Ivar standing in the doorway and the knife he was holding. She could feel the eyes of a group of kids out on the footpath, too close to her car for comfort. Like the kids Ivar had once rescued her from, but now out in the daylight. Bolder, more sure.

She would knock. It couldn't hurt. If it was the wrong house, it didn't matter. Zo was suddenly conscious that she was still muddy and bedraggled, but she forced herself up the stairs and to the door. Her knock sounded too loud, too presumptuous. But it provoked nothing. No stir of recognition from inside. She turned to go, deciding to walk up and down the street and attempt to get her bearings.

'Hello?' The man was old. Ancient. He wore faded trousers and a thin, worn jumper. Zo could see a glimpse of a white shirt through the fabric. His shoes were the best part of his ensemble. Polished, though the laces were thin and looked liable to break. He was unmistakeably Wirt. But a Wirt without the panache of the man she knew.

'Hi,' said Zo. 'I think we've met before—'

'I know who you are,' said Wirt. Zo smiled. Wirt liked her. He'd shown her his insects. 'You're after a room.' He turned and walked inside. His gait was as slow as it had ever been, but there was something about it that seemed less vigorous, stiffer. Zo followed him. The house had been turned into a warren of small rooms. They walked through an area that seemed to be a common lounge room; it was covered with discarded clothes and boxes and cigarette butts. The kitchen must be close by: Zo could smell old oil, the remains of something burnt and underneath that an ammonia whiff. Wirt began to climb the stairs at the back of the house. He was so slow that Zo felt that she should stop him. She'd come under false pretences; she did not want a room. But she said nothing and followed along after giving him a moment to gain something of a lead. A television was blaring from one of the rooms. A stream of advertising morphing into what seemed to be a soap opera. Nothing Zo recognised.

Two flights of stairs and then a small room at the back. There was a bathroom on the same level. Its sink was coated with mould and soap scum was visible even from the landing. An old toilet sat in its own compartment, cracked seat mocking Zo as she walked by.

Wirt held a door open for her and she squeezed past him into a room that was the smallest she'd ever seen. Room for a bed and a chest of drawers and little else. Zo could see a woman's shoe under the bed and discarded cosmetics on top of the drawers. Nothing was clean. Everything had developed its own patina of stains and dirt. The wallpaper was peeling, revealing an undercoat of pinkish paint over crumbling plaster.

Off to the side, grimy mesh curtains were pinned back from smeared windows. A torn insect screen appeared to be gummed to one window, although a corner was making its escape. The balcony – hardly that, a suspended piece of concrete and metal barely enough for one person – held a plastic fold-up chair and a full ashtray.

'I'll need a deposit,' said Wirt. 'Any damage'll come out of that. And two weeks in advance.'

Zo shook her head. She was close to tears, but she couldn't think of words that wouldn't offend Wirt. He must know. He must think this was dreadful. She thought of the man she knew. Impoverished but proud. Dapper. And his meticulously crafted creations. That man was worried about the possibility of mould. This man had suspended himself in it.

'No,' she said. 'This is not what I want.'

Wirt shrugged. 'Well, if you've better options,' he replied. The look on his face suggested that Zo had no other choice, that she was lucky to have a room at all.

Zo was first horrified and then ashamed of herself for being so fussy. She tried to persuade herself she could stay. She could clean it after all, make something of it. She shook her head.

'No, I'm sorry. I was looking for someone. Ivar.'

Wirt looked at her blankly.

'The man ... with the knife ... I saw him standing in the doorway earlier.'

Wirt looked at her again, assessing her interests and his options in them.

'Nobody here by that name,' he said at last.

'My mistake,' said Zo. She saw Wirt's look. Nothing here for you, it said. She turned, tried not to run as she went down the stairs and back through the house. Tried not to cry and, when she got to the car, not to tear off her clothes and remove the stench and the dirt from her person. She pulled out from the kerb, out and away, and she didn't care where. But the tears were making it hard to drive, stinging her eyes in that way tears sometimes would, and when she saw a spot to safely put the car, she pulled to the side of the road. She rummaged through her bag until she found tissues and a comb then sat for a few minutes with her eyes closed until she could breathe.

She was parked in front of a group of shops. Some sported faded signs that told of moves to better premises. One had a broken window and it loomed with a sense of further unpleasantness inside. But she knew the shop at the end of this group. Her café.

She got out of the campervan and brushed the worst of the drying mud away from her clothes. She paused for a moment, wondering if she could bear it if this shop was different too. If there was no barista with blue hair, or if he didn't recognise her. She had to try; it was the closest thing to home she could think of. The only possibility of refuge. She told herself a warm drink would be enough, that was all she could expect. She checked her wallet. The moth sat on her shoulders. It hadn't come into Wirt's house with her. This must be a good sign, the moth on her shoulder.

The cafe looked much as it always did. She recognised one

of the men behind the counter. He was making a large, thin pancake and covering it with some chocolate spread. He did not look up. A middle-aged, blonde woman took Zo's order. She was chatty and efficient, but she didn't know Zo. She could feel the woman assessing the mud on her clothes, the disarray of her hair. But when her hot chocolate was finally ready, she took it to the back of the room, found the place she thought of as hers and sat.

The drink was hot, but thin on chocolate and the milk was strange. But it was the best thing Zo had consumed all day and this was the safest, most reassuring place she had found in some time.

She kept thinking should go home; she kept remembering the wheeling cockatoos and the increasing jungle of the drive. Home might not exist anymore. It was better if she didn't know for sure. She finished her drink and nursed the mug to herself for a moment, keeping the warmth, hoping for more comfort and, perhaps, inspiration.

'I thought you might need tea.' Her barista sat down in front of her. His hair was plain black, no colours, but otherwise he looked the same. The tattoos swirled up his arms and tiptoed around his neck, telling their unreadable story. She was so glad to see him, she found it hard to answer.

'Yes,' she said at last. 'Yes, tea would be good. Thank you.'

The barista smiled as if Zo was being slightly ridiculous, slightly too effusive. He placed a beautiful, ornate teapot down on the table then leant over to a side cabinet and produced two matching cups. Had this cabinet had been there before? It seemed so solid, so completely part of the place. How could she have missed it? The moth flew over to it and settled gently.

The colours of its wings matched the wood.

'You know me, don't you? I mean, you recognise me ... from before.'

'Of course.' He picked up the teapot, poured a little tea into each mug, swirled the liquid around and then threw it out into Zo's empty hot chocolate mug. He poured again, this time with greater care.

The tea smelt of Kyra's garden. It was the kind of drink she would take out to her own back deck to watch the parrots. The barista picked up his mug and sipped. He was looking at Zo, watching her closely, but she didn't know what he expected. She picked up her own mug, aware of the specks of dried mud on her sleeves. She tried to let the tea infuse her with calm.

'How can I help?' he asked.

'Nothing is right.' The words spurted out of her. Although she had no way of explaining, she had to try. 'Everything should be better. Everyone should be better. Happier, less ... dirty. They should know who I am.'

'I know who you are.'

'Not you ... Everyone else ...'

'How can you be sure this is not the way things should be?'

'The house where I was staying, the house.' Zo gestured towards the small table where she was sure she'd seen brochures in the past. The table was there, but the only thing on it was a pot plant. Some kind of fig with a round potbelly. 'The house down the road where I was staying,' she continued. 'It's gone. And the people who lived there. People who I knew. I found them. Some of them. They don't know me.'

The barista took a long sip of tea. He held the mug in his

hands and watched the steam rising from the water.

'I met a ghost,' said Zo. 'He seemed real, but he can't be.'

'A ghost can be real.'

'I don't know what to do for them,' said Zo. 'If they need help, how can I give it? I have no idea what's needed.'

'The house must have called you for a reason.'

'The house? I thought it might be ...' She'd thought it might be Callum, but that seemed too foolish to say.

'The ghost?' Zo nodded. 'I don't think so.'

'But the house is gone.'

'The house is older than you.'

Old didn't mean it could appear and disappear at will, thought Zo. The barista lifted his mug and drained the last of the tea. Her time of refuge was almost over. She would have to leave and there was nowhere to go. She held on to her own mug, not wanting to drink the rest.

A glimpse of sun broke onto the street.

'The rain's stopped,' she said. But her words were muffled by a crowd of people bustling into the shop. Well-dressed, happy, ordinary people. They weren't beggars like Wirt, or full of despair like Tim.

'I should help.' The barista stood but left his mug and the teapot on the table.

'Thank you,'

He smiled, nodded, already away to deal with orders. Zo swallowed the rest of her tea.

She walked out into the sun and followed the footpath down the hill. The campervan could stay where it was for a bit. Everything seemed better now that the sun was out. Zo felt like skipping as if she was six years old again. When she came to Kyra's house she stopped. Everything was as lush and verdant as ever. A castle of green. But she continued down the hill, her footsteps growing even faster as the gradient of the hill steepened. There was the house. Old, uncared for, resplendently beautiful. The mud was gone, and the neglected garden was back. Zo rushed up the path to the front door and it swung open even as she put her hand to the wood.

Chapter Thirteen

Something inside was banging in the wind. Something small, perhaps a cupboard door. Zo walked through to the lounge room and saw that one of the windows wasn't latched properly. She climbed onto the couch which rested against the wall and lent out, grabbed the window, pulled it back and latched it. She was almost close enough to touch the outer leaves of the great, thick palm tree in the backyard. The base looked like the skin of an ancient reptile, with overlapping dusty, grey scales. She'd never noticed it before. She leant on the windowsill with her knees on the couch, looking out into the garden. It was in the same state as the house: signs of former grandeur, signs of neglect. Long grass had begun to overtake formal garden beds. There was no sign of the potted herbs Edda had talked about. But to the side of the palm tree, almost hidden by its trunk, was an area closed off by a rickety wire fence. Zo thought she could see a gravestone, though perhaps it was just a garden ornament, an old fountain.

Footsteps. Only Ivar. He looked tired.

'You making coffee?' he asked.

'I guess I could,' said Zo. She had no desire for more drinks.

'Don't worry. Make it myself.' He went into the kitchen and Zo listened to the clangs. She wanted to follow him, badger him with questions. She felt devastatingly shy. No question formed itself that didn't seem foolish.

When Ivar returned with coffee, Zo was still on the couch. He pulled up a chair from the dining table and she turned around so that her feet were back on the floor.

'Where've you been?' he asked.

'It's hard to describe,' said Zo.

'Try me.' Ivar took a sip of his drink.

'Last time I saw you,' began Zo. You were holding a knife, peeling some fruit in front of a run-down boarding house, she thought. 'You were showing me Callum's room.'

'And?'

'And he was there. I talked to him and then ... then I fell through the house into the mud, and it was as if it wasn't there at all.'

'So that explains the state of you,' said Ivar.

Zo nodded. 'I met you,' she said. 'Well, I saw you. But you didn't know me. And Tim and Wirt. Everyone was different. Everything was worse.'

'So you can see why I don't want to leave,' said Ivar. He took another sip of coffee, waiting for her to respond, daring her to challenge.

'I don't know what I can do,' said Zo. 'As soon as I touched his hand, everything fell away.'

Ivar shrugged. 'So you can't pull him back physically. Doesn't mean there's nothing else you can do.'

'You said it was a mistake I was here.'

'Probably, yes.'

'What happened to him?'

'Official take on it is drowned at sea. Whale Watch claims something underhand, some subterfuge. But there's no real evidence. Or none that's been made public. Bottom line: he went out to sea; he never came back.'

'So why is he here?'

'Why isn't he haunting the waves, communing with the ghosts of whales and sharks? This is his home.'

Zo sat, looking at the floorboards. 'I still don't know what to do.'

'Take a shower, put some clean clothes on, visit him again.'

'You want me to get dressed up for a ghost?'

'Wouldn't hurt.'

Zo stood. She felt like kicking his leg. Ivar was pushing her to do something, to be something that even he didn't understand. He wanted her to make things right, but he couldn't tell her how. All he could do was laugh at her.

'I'm too old for this,' she said.

'I know,' said Ivar.

Or not old enough, thought Zo. She was already walking out of the room, towards the stairs. She would have a shower. Become warm and dry and presentable. And then she would visit Callum again.

*

Outside Callum's room, Zo took a deep breath. She wanted to go in. She did. She wanted to solve whatever problem it was the house and this man had thrown her into. But she also needed to compose herself. A gentle hand touched her elbow.

'There's no need,' said Reuben.

His face was etched with thin lines Zo had never noticed before. He seemed perfectly sincere, perfectly sympathetic to her. 'It can't help,' he continued, 'and you will only be hurt.'

'I want to do something.' It seemed so feeble.

Reuben shook his head. 'You should go back home. Back to people who love you.'

Zo couldn't help but feel hurt. She didn't expect the inhabitants of the house to love her; they barely knew her. But now she'd been discarded as an outsider. 'I can't seem to get home,' she told Reuben. 'This seems to be the only way.'

Reuben held his head to the side, considering her. Zo noticed the splotches on his glasses and the grey in his beard. 'How long have you been here?' she asked.

'It's different for me,' he said.

'But why?'

'Because I have nowhere else to go. And this ... this is a haven. For me. And for Edda.'

'You don't want me to make things worse for you.'

Zo thought of the dismal life she'd seen Tim and Wirt leading. There had been no sign of Reuben or Edda, although she hadn't been there long enough to be sure. She couldn't tell him about it without seeming crazed. Though he seemed to know. They both turned as they heard Edda's heels on the stairs. They waited, made statues by her approach. Edda was wearing a deep red dress and her hair was up in a severe, beautiful bun. Her perfume made Zo think of dark furs and cigarettes, things she had never associated with Edda before.

Edda threaded her hand through Reuben's arm, although it seemed more that Reuben was leaning on her than the other way around. 'Let her try,' she said. 'Let her visit and see what happens.'

'But—' began Reuben. Edda shook her head, and he didn't even try to finish his objection. Edda had already dismissed the possibility that Zo could have any effect. For her this was entertainment, and easier than trying to dissuade her. More likely, Edda wanted to see Zo come to some harm, suffer in some way as she had done herself. There was a streak of maliciousness in the woman.

Zo pushed the door open and then, before either of them could comment, she walked into the room. She saw Edda's look of triumph, Reuben's sadness. It was only after she had closed the door that she turned to see who or what was inhabiting this space now.

The room was empty, just as it had been before. There was an armchair by the window and Zo tiptoed across the boards to it, every step cautious. She pulled the curtains across and yanked up the blind. It was old and dusty and the tassel at the bottom fell away in her hands. She tried to push the windows open, but they wouldn't budge. She sat in the chair and waited.

A small bookshelf sat under the window. Just three shelves. On top the bookcase sat a picture of a small, battered ship. Red teeth had been painted onto its front, making it appear a kind of man-made shark. But it was a small shark; even the old warship that was docked beside it looked so much bigger, so much more malevolent. A dragonfly landed on the bookshelf. Her own fly: it must have followed her into the room. She missed the moth, missed its organic loveliness but the fly was better, less fragile, more object than animal. It sat on something black and plastic, an old iPod if Zo wasn't mistaken. The haunting sound of whale song filled the room. Sometimes like a rusty trumpet, sometimes like the call of a drowning lover.

Zo closed her eyes and listened. She wished she could be more like these creatures. More sure of her place and her worth. She understood why Callum had wanted to protect them. This house thinks of itself as a whale. In need of protection; in need of care. Something landed on her arm with a flutter of wings and the light touch of tiny feet. Not her own fly, another creature. She opened her eyelids just enough to see that it was a moth, not the moth of her other journey, but something similar. She didn't want to disturb it.

She sat back in the chair, closed her eyes fully and let the whale song envelope her. Let those large creatures call to her as if she were under the water with them. All the while, more and more insects land on her. So many now that she didn't want to look. She was not afraid; she had chosen this, though she did not understand it. She imagined herself covered in the creatures, a mound of wings and fuzzy insect bodies. She felt one on her eyelid, its wings meshing with her eyelashes. They weren't hurting her, but they were taking something. She could not stop it now; it had to happen. She tried not to move, so that she wouldn't disturb them, so that it would be over quickly. A sob welled up in her, but she couldn't let it past her throat. She did not want to open her mouth. She did not want them inside her.

Chapter Fourteen

Zo stood at the bottom of the stairs. She seemed to be stuck there. This morning she'd put on a top with long sleeves and a skirt that reached down to her boots. She'd wound a scarf around her neck. Her whole body was covered with bites. Most were just small things, tiny, raised bumps, only noticeable because of their profusion. But others had become itchy and, because she'd scratched at them without thinking, they'd become large and red and raised. The clothes she'd been wearing yesterday were close to ruined; tiny holes were threaded through them. Her face wasn't too bad. She'd taken time with it, trying to soothe the bites that were there and covering them with foundation. She thought she was presentable enough to go outside, but now that she was near the door, she wasn't sure.

'Why are you wearing that get up?' Ivar was at the letterboxes. He had a cup of something in his hand, but Zo hadn't heard his footsteps.

She didn't know how to explain. She wasn't sure that she wanted to. She couldn't tell him the clothes were a form of camouflage.

Zo spread her hands. 'It suits my mood today.'

Ivar leaned towards her, took in her face. Zo was sure he noticed the bites.

'What is that shit you were just playing? I like the other one better.'

'Everyone likes Debussy.'

'And everyone hates that other stuff?'

'Messiaen. He's very well-known.'

'Doesn't mean he's not shit.'

Zo turned away. There was no point trying to bring Ivar around. Zo had tried to steady herself by playing the piano. But nothing had seemed right. She'd chosen something harsher, more in keeping with her mood. It hadn't helped. It wasn't even a complete piano piece. It was meant to be played with other instruments, but something about her state of mind had drawn her back to her student days, to a time when she had other musicians to play with. When she had hope and optimism.

'You going out?' Ivar seemed determined to torment her.

'No.' She'd barely coped with this interaction. 'I thought I might take a look at the back garden.' She'd remembered the half glimpsed grave now.

'Really?'

'Yes, really.' Zo could tell him what had happened. Could he guess? Did he know? Instead, she walked past him, out through the lounge room, through the kitchen and to the back door that Edda had used.

She drew back the lock and it moved easily through the metal hasps. The door itself seemed stuck for a moment when she pulled at it, as if the wood had swollen in wet weather. But soon enough she was out. Immediately in front of her was a paved area, more crooked bricks than pavers, and it was filled with pots containing Edda's herbs. Beyond that was grass and the wide, old palm tree. She walked towards it. The grass was still damp, and it had grown thick and wild. It wasn't until she was close to the palm that she saw the rusty, woven wire fence and the headstone. The fence was broken at the back; the grave was less protected than she had imagined. Tim was there. He'd spread out his cards in the place she imagined the actual grave would be, close to the headstone. He looked up as she approached and smiled. A cautious smile as if he thought she might now understand but wasn't sure.

Zo sat down on the grass in front of him, cross-legged like he was. Her skirt would get wet; already she felt the moisture seeping through to her skin. It was comforting somehow.

'Hey,' she said. Softly, not wanting to frighten him.

He reached over and touched her cheek. He was checking the bites, making sure that she had done what had been asked of her.

'Thank you,' he said.

'Will it help?'

'They can't bite, you know. Moths and butterflies.'

'Oh.' Zo reached up to touch her skin. She could feel the bumps and she had seen the raised welts on her body.

'Other insects might, spiders maybe. But the moths were just tasting you.'

Zo shuddered. She hadn't wanted to picture herself covered in moths, but when the thought crept into her brain she could bear it. But other creatures: spiders, worse things. That she did not want to think about.

'Why?'

'The house wants you to stay.'

'I can't stay. I'll do what I can, but—'

'Not you, a copy. An echo.'

'Like Callum?'

Tim nodded. Though he looked at her slyly as if to say, not quite like Callum. Callum was dead; the conviction washed over Zo. She imagined his body lying at the bottom of the ocean, surrounded by fish and bugs and tentacled things and she shook her head to take the image away.

'Who is that?' she asked, nodding at the headstone, more ready to take on the knowledge of the ordinary dead.

'Oh,' said Tim, 'no-one, in particular.' He looked at her again. Assessing her. 'Sometimes I imagine it's me,' he confessed.

Zo reached over, touched his knee. It was solid and real. His jeans were slightly dirty, his knee bone knobbly. He didn't eat enough. 'Why do you stay?' she asked. 'I understand what it gives the others. Even Ivar. And they're adults. They've made a choice.'

'Have they?'

'Yes, I think they have.'

'Maybe I've made a choice too.'

'You're too young,' said Zo. Before she thought, before she had time to stop herself. Tim didn't seem offended.

'I'm stuck,' he said.

'Because?'

He looked down, away from her gaze. 'Because I keep hoping. I keep thinking there's something more, something to see, something wonderful.' He looked up at her then, eyes pleading, faint tears brimming.

'You live in a house that belongs to a ghost. That somehow is still standing, still functioning. And you talk of it as if its somehow alive. That it makes ... copies of people. What more could you want than that?'

'I want it to happen to me.' Tim's voice was barely a whisper. 'She won't take me.'

'You're too young. That's all. That's nothing bad.'

'There's something wrong with me.'

'No, Tim, no. Look at me. I'm no-one. So very ordinary.'

'You have music.'

'Not really. Not properly. I might have if I'd tried. But I let it go. And now ... Now it's just a half thing. Something I used to do.'

'It doesn't sound like that to me.' Tim shuffled his cards and laid five out in a cross shape. 'Look,' he said, tapping the card on his right, 'it's always this one.'

The card showed a young man tied upside down. One leg was fastened to a tree by a vine, the other rested on the opposite knee so that it formed a triangle. He looked peaceful, happy.

'What card is that?' It wasn't a design that Zo recognised.

'It means I have to wait.'

Most of the cards were pictures: clouds and feathers and arrows that matched the symbols on the dice Tim owned. But the one at the top, the one closest to her, showed a naked woman kneeling. Her hair flowed around her like a cloak. She held a jug in each hand and was pouring water into a pond but also onto the grass. It was a beautiful card, but it reminded Zo of falling through the house. Of the mud and the spiderweb highlighted by rain drops.

'Sometimes,' she said. 'If you look for signs, all you can see are the things you already know. Sometimes you have to move, anyway. Even if it seems that nothing will go your way.' She took up the five cards, folded them back into Tim's pack. 'I never knew that. All my life I waited. I should have gone out after what I wanted.'

'What did you want?'

'I never really knew. That was the problem.' She stood up and brushed off her skirt. She stepped past Tim and walked up to the gravestone. The lettering was so weathered that it was unreadable. The stone was patchy and green on one side, but when Zo touched it, it felt cool and almost soft.

'Alice,' said Tim. 'Her name was Alice. She had a family too, but they all left her. I think that's why she likes you.'

'My family haven't left me.' Though here, standing on the grass, touching the gravestone, she felt as if they had. She took her hand away, held it to herself as if to prove she was real. 'Is it her, really, or is it the house?'

'I don't think there's much difference anymore,' said Tim. 'They don't want to drown.'

'I can't hold the water back, Tim. I can't stop it seeping through and rising higher. That's the way it is now; we all know that.'

'No,' said Tim, 'but if she thinks you can help, there must be a way. Maybe she just needs to become stronger.'

'She's taking what she wants.' And so should you, Zo thought, but did not say. She heard her name drift across the grass. She didn't want to respond to any call. Not right now. But she heard it again and realised that it hadn't come from the house itself. Someone was up in a tree several houses away waving to her frantically.

Zo laughed. It seemed so ludicrous, so wonderfully ordinary. 'Kyra?' she called as she ran across the garden.

'Yes! It's me.'

'What are you doing?'

'Mulberries! The tree is too large, but I can't bear to cut it down. Come help.'

Zo looked down at her clothes, aware of their unsuitability. But she ran anyway. She ran down the fence line, squeezed through a gap between an overgrown vine and the hot water system, out to the front garden and away. Running as if her life depended on it. If she'd been younger, she would have scrambled over the fences and through the backyards. But soon enough she was at Kyra's front door and then, realising Kyra was still in the tree, she moved self-consciously down the side of the house, past pots and vines and a tumble of gardening implements to Kyra's own backyard.

The tree wasn't as tall as she'd first thought. It was the slope of the hill that had delivered Kyra high up above the house and its garden.

'Hi,' she called.

'I didn't even know you could see your place. I haven't been up here for a while.'

My place, thought Zo. The old tumble of thoughts returned for a moment. Questions of money and logistics, how she might make things work if she stayed on. But they were faded and useless now. She didn't need to stay. How foolish she'd been to think that she might.

There were buckets full of fruit at the base of the tree.

Kyra bent down with a bucket in one hand, keeping her legs firmly wrapped around a branch. Her lips were stained purple.

'You're all dressed up,' she said when she handed the bucket to Zo.

Zo smoothed down the skirt. She couldn't think of a way to reply. Kyra lowered herself to the ground, using her legs as balance.

'Cup of tea?' asked Kyra. She took several of the buckets and Zo managed the rest.

They sat on the back steps. Kyra in her old, purple-stained clothes, Zo in her long skirt. She liked the way it drifted down over her legs, falling over the steps like a tablecloth. After a while, she lifted the edge, showed Kyra the bites.

'Oh, you poor thing. No wonder. That house, I'm sure it's full of insects. I'm surprised—' Kyra stopped, aware that she was close to upsetting Zo. Then she went down to the garden, plucked off a thick leaf from a spiky plant and ran the oozing edge over Zo's leg.

'Aloe,' she said. 'Best thing for it.'

Zo felt the gel soothing her skin, pulling it back to normality. 'Thank you.'

'Keep it,' said Kyra, offering her the leaf. 'And there's plenty more if you need it. Which it looks like you do.' She watched as Zo ran the leaf up one leg and then the other. Her legs were soothed, but the rest of her body had begun to itch in protest at its neglect. 'Why do you stay there?' she asked. 'I know it's none of my business, but ... it seems wrong.'

'They needed me for a while,' said Zo. 'But now... Now I think I can go home.'

'Good,' said Kyra. 'Your family must miss you.'

'They've been away,' said Zo. 'They'll be home soon.'

Kyra touched her arm lightly. 'You could always visit. Come with the others, work in the garden.'

Zo smiled. She didn't want to say yes; she couldn't imagine herself back. Not because of Kyra, but because of the house itself. Even now it seemed to be pulling away from her. Her reasons for staying seemed remote and slightly crazy. She did not understand the person she'd been for the past few weeks.

Kyra stood and Zo thought she'd offended her, but then she heard it, the faint sound of a baby's cry. 'I'll go,' she said. The women hugged. A goodbye.

Kyra turned, one foot inside her house. 'I'm glad you stayed, Zo. I'm glad to have met you.' And then she disappeared inside. Zo was happy, and teary and relieved all at once.

Coda

Zo's bag had been placed at the bottom of the stairs. Beside it was an old basket, filled with bits and pieces from her room. Her toothbrush. Shampoo. Spare clothes she'd bought. Nothing from the kitchen, despite all the food she'd left there. Zo felt mean at the thought of claiming it. Her t-shirt and jeans were carefully folded. They'd been mended, not in a rough, make-do way, but in row after row of beautiful lines and patterns so that they'd become art works, far more beautiful than before. Almost too precious to wear. Zo suspected Wirt's hand. A thank you, a reminder. On top of it all sat her dragonfly. She was glad of its plastic, artificial nature. She could not bear to see another insect, even one of Wirt's.

There was no-one around. She wanted to say goodbye. Wish them well, explain that she'd done all that she could do, though she did not understand it at all, but now she was leaving. It didn't seem right to walk any further inside.

Piano music drifted down the stairs and into the hallway. Zo couldn't place it. It was neither the Debussy nor the Rachmaninoff. Not even Messiaen. Something close, yet far away. She thought of the copy of herself, up in her room.

Would she visit Callum, have dinner with the others? Would she look after Tim? Mesh him in further to the house or encourage him to leave? She should have asked Kyra to help, but then she thought of her baby, Beattie. No, Kyra could not come here.

She gathered her bits and pieces. The front door was still open, and she stepped easily into the sunlight, down the crumbling stairs, up the faded path and through the gate.

The campervan was waiting for her. It had not been there this morning. Perhaps Ivar had driven it down. She saw the rust along one of the doors and she loved it as if it were the last ship home from a wartorn land. Perhaps it was. Soon she was on her way, out of the narrow inner-city streets, back over the bridges and home. She might visit again, with the girls, with Michael. But she didn't think so. She would be unable to explain, and if she had failed, if the house had crumbled to nothing, or had fallen into the water, she did not think she could bear to know.

Discover Luna Novella in our store:

https://www.lunapresspublishing.com/shop